I0743114

THE SINGING BOWL

Kini Collins

SPUYTEN DUYVIL

New York City

ISBN 978-1-959556-74-9

Library of Congress Cataloging-in-Publication Data

Names: Collins, Kini, author.
Title: The singing bowl / Kini Collins.
Description: New York City : Spuyten Duyvil, 2023.
Identifiers: LCCN 2023033452 | ISBN 9781959556749 (paperback)
Subjects: LCGFT: Novels.
Classification: LCC PS3603.O45436 S56 2023 | DDC 813/.6--dc23/
eng/20230905
LC record available at https://lccn.loc.gov/2023033452

as always, for Sue

Tell all the truth but tell it slant—
Success in Circuit lies
Emily Dickinson

Setting the last tie rod on her sculpture, Rob Morgan glowers at Mick's latest, pert and pretty in her black mini-dress, straight blonde hair flowing over her bony shoulders and thinks Jesus where does he find all these shrunk-down Joni Mitchells.

Your first solo show! the latest Joni cries with the fakest of fake interest. Who would have thought! You must be so nervous!

Rob mutters, If all the world's a stage, right there is one poor fucking player. Gallery assistant my ass.

No reason to be nervous, Mick answers for her. It's perfect, the perfect exhibit for opening the season. Rob's work is kick-ass. He slides his long arms into his leather jacket, straightens his skinny tie, red, to match his hi-tops.

Bile rises into her throat and Rob feels a familiar burning in her chest. She reaches to tuck her long brown braid behind her ear, still surprised at its absence.

the barbershop is empty. she goes in and sits in one of the oversized rotating chairs. the balding barber, black apron with combs and scissors in small pockets, waves her off, no girls. just cut it off, she says, cut all of it off. look, I told you, I don't do—she reaches in the tall cylinder of blue liquid, yanks out a pair of long pointed scissors, holds her braid out sideways and hacks it off. it sounds like sandpaper scraping a piece of wood.

she drops the braid on the floor. here, she hands
the scissors to the barber, handle end first, just
pretend I'm a boy.

With three clean shots of the electric drill Rob bolts
the metal strap to the floor. The latest Joni smirks at her,
secure in the knowledge that it may be Rob's show but
she will be the last one standing, the one Mick chooses
at the end of the night.

So we're all set then, Mick says, Yes?

They look around the long, narrow room. The spare
space radiates the we-don't-give-a-damn typical of lower Manhattan galleries in the early 70s. But the uneven
wooden floor has been wet-mopped, several bottles of
decent wine sit next to actual glass wine glasses on a
table in front of the chipped but newly-washed window.
Mick's space is finally on the map. Young for the gallery
game, he is becoming known for his finds. Although he
hasn't hit the big time, he is certain he will, and then
be able to expand to the cavernous spaces of the heavy
hitters. More than a few of his artists have been poached
to become someone else's New Young Thing.

The tallest sculpture, the one Rob has just finished
installing, stands in the center of the room—five others, free-standing in a row, about ten feet behind it. The
life-sized wooden figures, lined up shoulder-to-shoul-
der, resemble a church choir, or soldiers on patrol. The
track lights are angled to hit the pieces so they cast stark

shadows on the uneven plaster walls, across the painted tin ceiling.

Rob runs her hands up the back of the central piece, as if helping it to stand straighter, taller, then pushes on it, hard, side to side, front to back, making sure it rests secure. Built from discarded pier pilings scavenged along Twelfth Avenue, she has joined several together with wooden pegs before starting to carve. The simple figures are slender but somehow fierce. Mostly sanded to a smooth whiteness, the black of the tarred wood is visible in the spaces behind the knees, the insides of the elbows, under the chins—enough so that there is a faint odor of smoky, sour creosote, a slight taste of the brackish river water that had soaked the wood for years. The eyes of the totemic faces are closed, mouths open slightly as if beginning to speak. A wooden milk crate painted white is full of 8 penny finishing nails and sits at the feet of the sculpture, like an offering.

For Christ's sake! Rob yells, looking down into the crate. Do I have to do everything around here? Where's the fucking hammer?

The Joni looks blankly at Mick.

In the office, he snaps at her. With the tools? Second shelf.

She comes running back with a heavy wood-handled hammer, This one?

Rob snatches it from her, mumbles What a moron, and drops it into the crate. And the papers? The instructions? You did that at least?

Mick points to a pile of long strips—like you'd get in a fortune cookie—on the table next to the wine and says, We'll hand those to people when they come in.

Rob grabs one, reads out loud. Pick up the hammer. Pick up a nail. Pound it in. Pass the hammer. She crumples the paper, shoves it into the pocket of her dusty denim overalls. You think they'll get it? she says, mostly to herself.

Trust me, Mick says. The show is called *Disfigure*. Who wouldn't get it? It's a great concept, kiddo. Brings people into your process, lets them create the meaning of the piece. I've got press coming. Trust me.

The Joni gestures to Rob's stained overalls, the sagging sleeves of her dirty turtleneck. You're going to change?

Fuck you, Rob mutters. She picks up the hammer, plucks a nail from the crate, positions it on the sculpture, aimed directly at its heart. With two powerful strokes she sinks the nail into the hard wood. The small shiny head catches the light.

Mick yanks the cord on the shade covering the door. It rolls up with a slap. He spins the lock, props the door open with a wedge of wood, says over his shoulder, At least go wash your face, he tells her, comb your hair.

Fuck you too, she starts to say, then remembers.

they get off the escalator at the museum. Mick points, there, that's what I want you to see. the

Giacometti. Rob steps close, leans in for a better view. I only ever saw his stuff in pictures, she says. it's amazing, like a skeleton, but so, I don't know, all there. Mick nods, good, good description. now look at the Henry Moore. yeah, she says, same there-ness, totally different style. I see, she murmurs. so how's it going, he asks, with that wood you've been collecting? not bad, not sure. had a weird idea, what if I made one that people helped finish. people who? the viewers. helped how? I don't know, it's probably a stupid idea. he shakes his head, no, kiddo, never quit on anything until you work it through. trust yourself. I do. you'll get there.

Yeah, alright, she says to Mick, I'll get cleaned up.

Later that night Rob lurks at the gallery door. She has made an effort, washed her hair, put on clean jeans, a clean black turtleneck. She even went and bought a new jacket, a green army surplus jacket, strong front zipper, lots of pockets. The gallery is full of casually well-dressed people, deliberately dressed-down artists. Mick is holding forth, his head of jet black curls shaking as he makes an important point, smiling fully and sincerely at a would-be, hoped-for buyer, all with his arm draped around the Joni's shoulder. Rob hears the hammer, some grunts of satisfaction when the nail is hit squarely, sinks well and deeply into the wood, a few squeals of excitement accompanied by tentative taps. Her downstairs neighbor, Seymour, has walked over with her. In his early fifties, he is a bear of a man, not overly tall, just this side of obese, with a full bushy beard and a nearly bald head. He's the only other inhabitant of their building. As the unofficial super he is somehow able to keep everything mostly working, jury rigging the elevator, the antiquated plumbing, the not-up-to-code electrical system. He's got the first and second floors, the third and fourth are used for storage for some textile company—nobody ever comes or goes—Rob is up top, on the fifth.

Before Mick spots her she says, I think I'll take a pass.

Seymour nods, Too big a big night?

Yeah, I'm a behind the scenes kind of person. Hey, thanks again for letting me use your truck to haul that wood from the river.

He pats her on the back, says, An unused truck is a waste of metal.

Let me know what you think of the work. As she heads off she reaches into her jeans pocket, cups the knife that fits perfectly in her hand, the knife she is never without.

don't lose this Robin, her mother says when she presses it into her palm, it was my father's. the red casing is scratched, the grey cross mostly worn off. the knife seems huge in Robin's small hand. see, her mother says, you pull the blades out like this. and see, there's scissors, a saw, even a pair of tweezers. you can do anything with this knife. that guy comes back, that last blow job she gave in Tompkins Square Park. he comes back as she is finishing a carving, the knife open in her hand. he sits next to her, silent, like most of them. she thinks he wants her to do it again but he grabs her by the hair, slams her head against the park bench, starts to pull her into the bushes. the knife in her hand is open, the bird she had been carving falls to the concrete. she lashes out, slices his arm. he screams, releases her head. she runs, holding the knife away from her body. rides the subway back and forth, from Union Square to Far Rockaway. it takes a couple of weeks but she finally goes into Mick's gallery—she had passed it more than twenty times—peeked in the window at the artwork, kept walking, sure she wouldn't be welcome. she shows him her birds, birds with bowl-like bodies, carved from tree branches. he can't believe that she made them with just a Swiss Army knife. and he laughs when she throws him that line from The Winter's Tale—Though I am not naturally honest, I am sometimes so by chance. he buys the birds, saves her life.

The following week at breakfast in Fanelli's, Mick says, Listen. This from Stevenson. This is terrific. Listen, "Taylor does it again. He opens the fall season with work by another unknown. Rob Morgan's work is classic yet risky, vulnerable but powerful. Having the public participate in the realization of one of her pieces is, far from a gimmick, a brilliant stroke. It is difficult to believe that Morgan, at only twenty years old, can evince such sophistication. And sensitivity. She is a strong new talent and the show is sure to be a sell out."

Rob lights a cigarette. I'm taking that as not a sell-out sell-out but a sell out?

I told you, didn't I? Where the hell did you go? People need to see you.

I stayed long enough. Saw that nobody fucked things up.

You have to meet them, you know.

Nah.

Especially the buyers. You have to play the game. I need you to.

Where's your latest?

Mick takes a big bite of toast, shakes his head, says, Not gonna work out.

Imagine my surprise, she thinks. So are they, she asks. Selling out?

He nods. All but one. The damaged piece was the first to go. Great craft in the assembly, kiddo. It held up even with all the pounding. You need to see it before it's shipped.

So I'm rich?

Depends on your definition of rich.

What's my cut?

About two grand. Maybe twenty-five hundred.

That's it?

Jeez, Robbie. I've been floating you for a while.

What am I, a tugboat?

It adds up.

Yeah, alright, I guess, she says curling her hands into fists, thinking, hell it beats giving blow jobs. She lays her palms on the sticky table top, whispers, I don't like being seen. What if somebody from—

There's been nobody. In close to two years. That guy from the squat? He's not looking for you, if he's even still alive. You didn't do anything illegal, did you?

She shrugs, No but I did sic the cops on them.

So maybe change your hair again. But this is a good style, you are short enough to pull off the pixie look.

Fuck you, she says with a laugh then runs her hands along the nape of her neck, feeling her mother's hands, her soft voice saying You do it now, Puck, side over center side over center.

Mick forks the last corner of cinnamon bun, offers it to her. The show's a smash, he says. Your work is good, really good. I knew they would love it.

She starts to push the fork away, then ignoring the

tightness in her stomach, takes the bite. Anybody saying you gave me the show because we fuck?

Not with the sales you racked up, kiddo. Besides, who the hell cares. But I need you to visit a couple of buyers. I lined up two, one mid-town, one on the upper west side.

Ah come on, I—

Don't whine. It's part of the game. You ditched the opening, this is the least you can do. And you should maybe move.

Fine, I'll see your buyers, but I'm not moving. I wanna stay on Greene Street. Donald and Maria said I could use the loft until they get back.

Really, you should check out Westbeth. Better spaces, better networking.

Nah. I'd have to buy tools, all my own stuff. Using Maria's is better.

But Westbeth is—

Too far uptown. Too artsy.

You'd fit right in, Rob Morgan. Nobody artsier than you right now.

She scoffs, sops up the last bit of egg with a corner of toast, pops it in her mouth. So you wanna fuck?

Mick stubs out her smoke, cups the back of her head, kisses her on the forehead. Is your elevator working?

Yeah. For now.

You sure?

You want to come over or what?

Yeah, it's been a while.

She shrugs, Not my fault.

Rob is proud that she's finally got enough so that Mick doesn't have to pay her rent this month. She knocks on Seymour's door, yells, Got the money. Should I just put in the mailbox?

No, no, Seymour opens the door wide. Come on in.

Wow wow wow wow wow, Rob says and whistles. There must be a thousand jars here.

Nine hundred fifty-four.

It's like walking into a private hardware store. On one side of the room, for at least thirty feet, are shelves running from the floor up to the fourteen foot ceiling. Each shelf is completely lined with lidded glass jars—jelly jars, pickle jars, peanut butter jars—each with a strip of masking tape listing what is inside. Tiny brass screws. Tiny galvanized nails. Five-tooth sprokets. Eleven-tooth sprokets. Plastic doll arms. Two-inch washers. Fender washers. Chrome crap. Watch bands. Clock faces.

Aren't you worried they'll fall off?

Building is pretty solid. No big earthquakes in Manhattan. He points to the floor, Miles of schist down there.

Your studio. So clean, organized. So different from Maria and Donald's.

I like knowing where everything is. And I keep the dirty stuff in the basement.

Rob points to the opposite wall, Grates on the windows?

He shrugs. Were here from when it was a factory. Feels safer.

First floor, I get it. She wanders to a long wooden table under the windows. These tins, she points to a stack of painted tins, are these from Altoids? You paint them?

He hands her a tin, Open it.

The entire inside, lid included, is covered with bits of metal, glass, fabric. She lifts it close to her face to see better. I can't—

No, no, he says, hold it away, like arm's length.

Holy crap, she says. From a distance a scene resolves. All the tiny pieces form a perfect NY skyline—buildings, streets, even a bridge across the river. She hands it back to him, This is amazing!

He shrugs, sets the tin back on the table. Nah, not so amazing. But tourists love them. Sell them for twenty bucks in Washington Square Park.

You could get a lot more in a store or a gallery, for sure.

No fun that way.

Can I look at more?

Maybe later. You want tea? Come in back.

Did you put up this wall?

Was already here. The offices were here, back here.

Holy double crap, Rob says with a laugh as she steps into the back room.

There are eight open spaces, set along the walls like rooms in a train, each about ten by ten feet, four on each side. The bottom half of the walls separating the rooms are polished mahogany panels, the top has etched glass in wooden frames up to about ten feet toward the ceiling. There are no doors to the rooms, just an opening out onto a center hallway.

Open offices so the bosses could keep tabs, Seymour says. But look at that workmanship in the wood, the glass. Even for just the clerks, bookkeepers.

Seymour has furnished each space differently, like in an apartment. A living room, dining room, several bedrooms, all filled with antique furniture, beautiful lamps, hand loomed rugs. Two of the rooms are set up like a library, bookshelves line the walls, an overstuffed chair and a small desk in each one. At the very back, the space opens up to a kitchen, the bathtub in the corner, similar to Rob's.

I'm still working on the back end, Seymour says.

All this furniture?

My old house was a lot bigger, he says. Needed to keep it. You like Lapsang Souchong?

Whatever that is, sure. And here, she takes an envelope out of her jeans pocket, hands it to him.

He takes the envelope, sets it on the shelf next to the jar of tea, Right on time you are, thank you.

Maybe sometimes you can show me more of your work?

Maybe.

How about the elevator? Can you teach me how to fix it?

Seymour beams. Yes. That.

Late at night, Rob often finds herself on West Tenth Street between Fifth and Sixth Avenues. She lingers on the curb in front of her old house. It's been almost ten years but it hasn't changed much. A few more chipped bricks, still no window boxes, no fancy iron railings, the brass door knocker shaped like an owl now missing its striker plate. She tries to fall into the memory—standing on the stoop, her mother on the sidewalk playing Titania, Rob doing Puck's final speech—So, good night unto you all. Give me your hands, if we be friends, And Robin shall restore amends—entertaining the neighbors on muggy summer nights. The cold of the concrete seeps into her bones but she stays, willing that memory to the forefront but only ever getting this one.

the change rattles into the tool booth basket. the car picks up speed. he sticks his lit Lucky Strike between his teeth, rolls the window back up, checks the rear-view, then joins the line of cars disappearing into the tunnel. the car is stuffed – front seat with cardboard boxes, Robin and Jonah in the back, crammed in behind him by a bunch of suitcases. Robin holding Jonah's head in her lap to keep it from flopping side to side, her head against the window bouncing up and down. speed up, slow down, slam on brakes. he curses the traffic, weaves in and out. the smoke from the cigarette, the swaying of the car. her

stomach full of butterflies. she knows they are
leaving their home but she can't make it make
sense, it hurts to remember so she begins counting, counting numbers in her head, blocking out
the feelings, blocking out everything. he cracks
the vent window and flicks the cigarette out. she
ducks as sparks shoot past her face then sits up
taller, strains to see it. but the blue and yellow
tile that spells NEW YORK/NEW JERSEY goes
by in a blur.

The uniformed doorman checks a list, makes a quick phone call, smiles a phony smile and ushers Rob and Mick into the black granite-floored lobby.

So this is where people who can afford my sculpture live, Rob thinks. What's this guy's name again? she asks Mick.

Harold Markham. He wanted the central piece, the one the viewers nailed, but it was already sold. He really wanted to meet you.

The sleek mirrored elevator takes them up to the 52nd floor. The door to Markham's apartment is open, Rob and Mick walk into a wide, open room, floor to ceiling windows all around, polished concrete walls, sleek metal and glass tables, black leather couches and chairs. Rob goes over to the southwest corner.

How the hell does he heat this place, she thinks but says, I've never been so high up, made my ears pop.

You can see all the way to New Jersey, Harold tells her.

Why would you want to do that, Rob mutters, but nods and smiles. Amazing view, truly.

Harold hands Mick and Rob tall glasses of sparkling water. They walk to the north side of the room. Rob's sculpture has been set on a low black plastic pedestal, lit from an overhead light.

What you think? Harold asks, good spot?

Mick nods, Yeah, great lighting.

It maybe doesn't need the pedestal? Rob says quietly.

I really wanted that other one, Harold says. I was thinking. Maybe you could take this back to your studio and pound in some nails? Like the other one?

Rob spins toward Harold, Mick puts a hand on her shoulder

I don't think Rob would be—

I'd be happy to pay, pay whatever.

Nah. Nah. It's not set up for that, Rob says, slipping out from under Mick's hand. It wouldn't take the pounding. I'd have to re-do the entire inside.

I can pay. Can't you change it?

No. I can't, Rob says. The one with the nails, that was, it needed other people to make it work. That was what it meant.

But I said I'd pay—

And I said no.

Harold sighs, I guess that's it then. I can put it in storage.

Why did you buy it if wasn't what you wanted?

I assumed you'd fix it, change it.

So you're just going to store it?

He nods. Until I decide to sell it.

Rob looks at Mick, says, What the hell?

Mick nods his head, Common practice for smart collectors, he says. Once you're better established and the prices for your work go up, Harold can take it to a dealer for resale.

And I get nothing?

It's legal, Harold says with a laugh, no law against it.

How about if I just pound on it now?

That's funny Rob, Mick laughs a nervous laugh.

So what do you do? Rob asks Harold.

Arbitrage. It's a kind of trading—

Yeah yeah. I know. It's that thing where you bet against yourself.

Harold takes a sip of his water. Smart kid, he says to Mick.

Maybe we should be headed out? Mick shepherds Rob toward the door. Harold, great to see you. I'll let you know when Rob has her next show.

Do that, Harold says with a smirk. Always in the market for work that appreciates.

A few days later Rob and Mick stand in front of the stately building near the corner of Riverside Drive and 84th Street. Above the filigreed metal door, at the apex of a granite arch, sits a slightly cross-eyed gargoyle. The panel to the right of the door has twelve names, just two for each floor. Mick presses the bell for 6A, the return buzzer sounds immediately.

How old do you gotta be to live in this building, Rob grouses. This is it, she says to Mick, the last one I'm doing.

I get it, Mick says.

What's this one's name? she asks Mick as they get on the elevator.

Grace Shapiro.

She bought the hammered one?

Right off the bat. Didn't even ask the price.

All I have to do is be nice, shake her hand and we can go?

Jesus, Rob. Make an effort. A new client for me, a collector for you. Nice is the minimum. She's not like Markham.

That's a low bar.

The elevator opens onto a small foyer. A round table sits exactly between the mahogany doors labeled 6A and 6B, a pewter lamp with a Tiffany shade casts a range of greens across the polished marble floor. Petals from dying pink lilies stain the white tablecloth with blood-colored pollen.

The door to 6A opens. Rob takes a deep breath, gets ready to heave a big sigh, then stops, whispers to Mick, Why the hell didn't you tell me. The woman at the door looks absolutely nothing like the wizened wealthy old lady she expected. Grace Shapiro, long and lean, somewhere in her late 30s, wears her curly black hair cropped tight to her head, creased bell bottom jeans, expensive leather boots, a white button-down shirt open over a black leotard.

I'm so glad you came, Grace smiles. I need your help, to place the piece. Leading them through a short, narrow hallway, Grace points to Rob's sculpture standing against a wall, its cloth wrapping lying at its feet.

The living room, its twelve-foot ceiling with tear-drop chandelier, is dominated by a modern yellow ocher couch that compliments the antique tables and chairs. Oriental rugs on the oak parquet create strong color patches on the floor, windows uncovered by drapes open onto a view of the river. Several small paintings hang between floor-to-ceiling bookshelves. A hallway to the kitchen has four doors leading to more rooms. The soft hiss of the radiators makes the warm room even warmer.

Holy crap, this place is huge, Rob says.

Grace laughs. Was my grandmother's, all of this, except the couch. The building is rent controlled or I would never be able to afford it.

Your collection is wonderful, Mick chimes in. Is this actually a Degas drawing?

Again, Grace waves it off, Not my doing. Grandparents had really great taste.

And some serious cash, Rob says.

Mick elbows her.

No, it's true, Grace laughs. The sole inheritor, that's me. She walks up to Rob, sticks out her hand, It is so great to finally meet you. I needed to see who made this extraordinary sculpture.

Rob thinks, Why, would it be less extraordinary if you never met me, but she takes her hand, shakes it. Before she can let go, Grace lays her other hand on top of Rob's. Her hand sandwiched between Grace's, Rob feels a jolt, a shot of heat run up her arm.

As she withdraws her hand she smiles, nods. I'm glad it went to a good home.

Grace gestures to the room, So where do you think?

Rob shrugs, That's Mick's department. I just make them.

Mick steps back toward the entry hallway, scans the room for a bit then points to an empty space between two bookcases. Over there, I'd say. The light from across the room will enhance the shadows on the face.

Grace nods, Yeah, and the nail heads will really shine.

All that glitters *will* be gold, Mick laughs.

It's glisters, Rob says, not glitters.

You know that? Grace says, the Prince of Morocco's speech about Portia? She leans toward Rob, smiles, Nobody gets that right. A Shakespeare lover, and a great sculptor?

Rob scoffs.

Why are you so familiar with the bard?

My mother. We used to do speeches. Just for fun.

So you're named after Robin Goodfellow?

Woah! Only one person ever got that.

Grace looks into Rob's eyes. Not much of a leap, she says. Chopped hair, not too tall, willing to stir up some shit. Who else but Puck.

Rob, maybe for the first time in her life, blushes.

She takes one of Rob's hands, turns it over, smiles. And you've got great hands.

Yeah, yeah, Rob mumbles but smiles back as she shoves her hands into her pockets. If you say so.

So, Mick walks between them, should we try it in that space? Rob, give me one of those great hands.

Yeah, yeah, Grace says. I like it there. Maybe a little to the left?

The sculpture fits, fits in the room with the modern/antique mix, with the age of the building, with its proximity to the river where the piers used to stand. They look for a few minutes, in silence.

It does matter, Rob says under her breath.

Rob? Mick asks.

Where it is, it matters where it is.

Grace pats her on the shoulder. It belongs there. Belongs right there.

Rob turns, looks up at Grace.

Mick steps back, We don't want to take up too much of your time, I think we should be heading out—

So soon? Grace says.

Rob nods, It was great to meet you.

Hey, Grace says quickly, are you OK with amateur productions? A friend is Tamora in Titus Andronicus on Friday. Might be awful, but I promised. You want to come?

Titus? I've never seen that performed. Maybe, I'll have to check.

As they walk to the apartment door Grace hands her a leaflet, Here's the address. Maybe see you there?

Mick goes out the door, presses the button for the elevator. Rob, you coming?

Rob stuffs the paper in her jacket pocket she turns to Grace. So what's your favorite tragedy?

Grace smiles. The Scottish play. No contest.

Rob whispers, When shall we two meet again?

Grace holds the door so that Rob has to pass under her outstretched arm and whispers back, When the hurlyburly's done, when battle's lost and won.

Walking east from Riverside Drive Rob says, Well hell. I thought you wanted to stay for a while?

Mick puts his arm around her shoulders. Not good to get too friendly. You did good, kiddo. Are you going to that show?

Rob steps out from under his arm. Maybe. You wanna go too?

He shakes his head. Nah, nah, not my thing. Is your elevator working?

Yeah! It got stuck but I was able fix it. Thanks to Seymour.

Holy crap, Rob says when she and Grace leave the theater. Really?

Grace laughs, Nothing holy about it. Just plain crap. She bumps Rob's hip, slides her arm around her shoulder. Thanks for sitting it out with me.

Rob adjusts her stride to match Grace's.

To be fair, Grace goes on, it couldn't have been easy to put on a play with ten murders, three rapes, cannibalism and insanity.

And an even bigger death count than Macbeth, Hamlet and Richard III put together. Jesus, wasn't there a whole lot of emoting going on.

It's a theme worth exploring though.

How to bake your enemies into a pie? It should come with recipes.

Grace leans into Rob. Revenge, how stupid the cycle of revenge is. What emulation can result in.

What's that?

When you want to up the ante. Not only want revenge but go over the top, to outdo the original act. Titus kills her son, Tamora wants revenge, but not just an eye for an eye, she wants to obliterate Titus.

And ends up eating her kids and being fed to the lions. Hey, we're not too far. Wanna see my studio?

Now?

Better three hours too soon than a minute too late. Yes?

And she knows the comedies too, Grace laughs. Can't now, early appointments. How about I come on Friday?

Corner of Greene and Prince. About 7? I'll wait for you downstairs, I'm buzzer-less.

Rob's neighborhood, named for one of its boundaries, had housed light industry and sweat shops in five-story buildings with huge windows, many fronted with intricate cast iron facades. When electricity became cheap, the companies fled the city leaving the beautiful, naturally-lit structures empty until discovered by artists. Still illegal to live in most of the buildings, the area is zoned as a commercial district—no regular trash pickups, police patrols or other city services—Soho is not on most people's radar.

Rob watches the taxi pull up in front of her building. She feels an excitement that she tamps down thinking, A taxi. There's a subway a block away. Why did I think this was a good idea.

Grace gets out of the cab, scowls as she side-steps a pile of dog shit, sees Rob, waves and smiles.

Rob tosses her cigarette into the gutter, Hey. Good to see you.

Sorry to be late. Traffic was pretty bad.

Elevator out of commission. Sorry.

Their steps ring loudly on the metal stairs.

Grace huffs and puffs, Top floor, huh?

Keeps me young—

You're just a kid!

she's just a kid, Maria says to Mick. Donald adds, and a little sketchy. and she's not deaf, Rob says. Mick laughs, she's fine, she's funny. she just needs a place and maybe some help. help how? Maria maybe you can show her your tools? I think she's really talented. look what she did with just a swiss army knife, for god's sake. Maria runs her fingers over the small bird, smiles. but it's green wood, she says, it'll crack when it dries. Rob steps close to them. it's a statement if it cracks, about everything cracking, nothing lasts. Donald roars, and she's great at bullshit! I love her. where did you find her? she came wandering into the gallery, Mick says, about a month ago. where are you living now? Donald asks. farther east. how far? Seventh and D. Donald murmurs, nothing there but dope squats. I'm not a junkie! Rob yells and turns to leave. never mind. I'm fine where I am! Maria stops her, it's OK kid, we're traveling for a while, maybe a couple of years, you want a sublet? how much? I'll cover it, Mick says, for a while.

Damn, Grace exhales as Rob unlocks the three dead bolts on the heavy metal door on the landing, I thought my place was big. You've got the entire floor?

Yeah. Come this way, we'll go in back. Watch your step.

In the dim cave-like room, Grace takes in the mismatched shelving crammed with books, magazines, old cameras, unidentifiable pieces of glass, jars full of screws, nails. Long, heavy metal tables sit against one wall, piled with blocks of wood, tools hang on the wall behind them. Ropes and extension cords suspend from the ceilings. Shallow plastic tubs nest on the floor, gallon jugs of some clear liquid sit under the tables. The windows running along the entire side wall are covered with tacked up newspapers that filter the incoming light and cast oddly-shaped shadows on the uneven wooden floor.

At the east end of the loft, a huge red velvet theater curtain, complete with tassels and fringe, separates the two sides of the loft. Beyond it, the windows at the back end are bare, daylight streams through the hundred year old glass. The clawfoot bathtub in the corner, towels draped on its sides, calls to mind a hippopotamus. Behind it, a painted door leads to a small room housing a toilet. A green Coleman propane stove sits on a solidly built table made of scavenged 2X4s and the small tin sink beside it is hooked up to a maze of copper and plastic pipes that lead into the floor. A battered fridge hums, vibrates. Stained and scarred, a butcher block table and five mis-matched chairs sit in the center of the space. Venting out a small side window that leads to an air shaft is a behemoth of a wood stove. Broken pieces of pallets and scraps of lumber are strewn around the tiled apron. A cast iron kettle hisses quietly on top.

Am I in a play? Grace asks. Through the curtain into a cabin in the woods? You use that stove? That's how you heat the whole place?

Just this part in the back. No need to heat the studio. I stay warm working.

Aren't you afraid?

Of?

Fire?

Nah. I like fire.

Grace points to the huge mahogany sleigh bed covered with layers of blankets and quilts along the north wall of the loft and laughs. You playing the Princess and the Pea?

Isn't that great! Has been in Donald's family forever.

She hands Rob a bottle of wine and a corkscrew. Do you?

Yeah, thanks! Be good with dinner. I made chicken cacciatore.

And she cooks! How do you do that in all this mess?

It's not a mess, they're artists, Donald and Maria. Artists have to have a lot of stuff. He's a photographer, she works in wood.

Like you?

She taught me a lot. How to use her tools. What woods could do what.

So where else did you study art?

High school.

No college?

Do you have a job?

Grace laughs, You think I'm rich because of my apartment? I work my ass off. I'm a clinical psychologist.

Rob nods, not completely sure what that means. She uncorks the wine, pours some in two bent metal coffee cups.

So we really are camping.

It's all I've got.

Just kidding. I'll bring you some glasses, it'll taste better. Are you from the city?

Until I was about ten, then we moved. Rob strikes a pose, recites, Crowns in my purse I have, and goods at home, And so am come abroad to see the world.

I hate that play.

Me too. But it's a good speech. Definitely was no experience to be found at home.

A farm?

Rob cracks up. Worse. A suburb.

Did your mother teach you to cook?

Nah. She died. That's why we moved.

That's awful.

Yeah, it was a terrible suburb.

Rob. Do you always makes jokes to deflect?

You're really good at that psych thing, aren't you? I never even told Mick that.

Is he your boyfriend?

Not even a little! He sells my sculpture, helped me get started. I like him.

But do you like him like him?

What are you? Twelve years old? Like I said, he helped me. Why do you think I am from New York?

You have an edge, always on that edge. Grace wanders to the front of the loft, studies some portraits pinned to the drywall. Is this?

Rob nods. Yeah. That was her.

These are exceptional drawings. When did you do them?

I didn't, don't remember. When I was still in school.

Grace points to a cloth covering a large form. New?

Not now. Time to eat. It's warm enough out. Let's go up to the roof. I love it up there. She opens the rickety window, props it with a 2x4, puts forks and knives, the wine and cups in a cloth bag, slings it on Grace's shoulder. Take this stuff and go on up, I'll get the food. And a blanket.

Is it stable?

Are you kidding? This fire escape has been here a hundred years.

That's what I'm afraid of.

Trust me. It's like my second home.

The sun is starting to set, the beginning of golden hour. They sit on milk crates at a cut-down wire spool table. Rob drops the blanket next to Grace, hands her a plastic bowl full of steaming chicken and rice.

You could actually see the river if it wasn't for that water tank, she says. Not as good as your view.

Grace takes a bite, says Hey, this is really good.

And that is so surprising?

No, no, Grace says as she pours more wine into the cups, just really pleased.

I've been cooking my whole life.

So how old are you?

What else? Twenty-one.

At the bar, I'm sure. But really. When were you born?

What are you, the bartender?

Just curious. About who it is that I find so interesting. That I like so much.

Rob takes a big swig of wine, thinks, you like me me or sculptor me. So what is it, she asks, what do you like so much?

Fishing for compliments?

Just curious. You, me, different worlds, aren't we?

Maybe that's what I like.

So you're slumming?

Look, Grace starts to stand, if you're not interested—

No stay, please. I'm just being an idiot. Really, I want you to stay. So tell me, she says, what's with the Shakespeare?

Grace settles back on the milk crate, takes a sip of wine. My grandmother. She was an actress. Always spouting it.

I never knew any of my grandparents.

Not always a bad thing. One of mine was great, my father's mother, but the other one used to lock me in the closet.

How come?

She was bat-shit crazy.

Is that a professional term?

Grace laughs. Today she would be diagnosed as a paranoid schizophrenic. But she came by it honestly.

Rob shakes her head.

She was a survivor. Concentration camp.

Oh, Jesus, Rob whispers.

No, not Jesus, Grace says. She was Jewish.

Rob relaxes, falls back into banter. Who's deflecting now?

Grace leans over the table, says, I think you know why I'm here.

Of course. For my world class cooking.

She takes Rob's face in her hands. Tell me you're at least eighteen.

She says, Way past eighteen, thinking, Jesus, I'm almost twenty-one.

Have you ever been? She gestures to herself, to Rob.

Yeah sure.

You want to know what I like about you? It's, don't take this the wrong way, it's like you are not one thing, like you're somewhere between, some of both. Not femme, not butch. I don't usually go for butch. But you are different. You are so physical, so at home in your body—

I get it, Rob cuts her off. I get it.

Grace reaches down, picks up the blanket, walks around the table and drapes it around them. Have you ever? Up here?

Although Rob has, she lies, smiles, says, First time for everything.

Seymour wraps a towel tight around Rob's bicep. For this we gotta go to the ER.

It's not that bad. I just cut it on a nail. All it needs is a band-aid.

He holds up the rusty nail she had pulled from a pier piling. This one? Can give you tetanus. You ever have a tetanus shot?

I don't know.

You wanna talk?

What?

It can lock your jaw.

Some people might be happy about that.

Just get in the truck.

Bellevue ER is hopping. Rob's arm has stopped bleeding, the towel crusty with dried blood. She wants to leave. Seymour insists she see a doctor.

I hate hospitals, she spits out. When were you last in a hospital?

First time for me, Seymour says. I was born at home.

How do you know about the ER?

He says in a deep voice, Man, woman, birth, death, he makes a figure eight with his fingers, infinity.

Say what?

From the TV.

Ben Casey?

I like the old guy, Dr. Zorba. Just sit quiet, they'll come soon.

she wakes to Jonah screeching, Coach screaming her name. in the kitchen Jonah is leaning on
the cabinet, cradling his arm, egg yolk splat-
tered on his shirt, the floor wet with slimy water.
Coach is standing over him, an empty frying pan
pulled back like a baseball bat. Jonah's arm is
turning colors, streaks of red and white from his
wrist to his elbow. what did you do? she yells at
Coach. why is he making my breakfast? Coach
yells back. Jonah is moaning, staring at his arm.
she pushes him to the sink, turns on the tap. put
it under the water. cold water. that's what she always used. Coach tries to get between Robin and
Jonah. she snarls. he lowers the pan, takes one
step back. I didn't mean it, Jonah says, I didn't
mean to break the egg. I just wanted to help you.
he starts shivering, the water on his arm is useless. we have to go to the hospital—no! Coach
roars. it's not that bad. I will call the cops, she
says. he lifts the pan. I will call the cops, she
says again. Coach scowls, get him in the car. she
sits in the back with Jonah, keeps a wet cloth
on his arm. he has stopped shivering, is crying
softly. a few blocks from the hospital Coach pulls
the car over, puts it in park, keeps the motor
running. he turns and looks at them in the back-
seat. so what happened. Jonah? Jonah struggles
to speak, finally says, I was making breakfast,

a poached egg, and I tripped with the pan of hot water. Robin? she and Coach lock eyes. I overslept, she says. I was supposed to make breakfast and I overslept. didn't see what happened. he puts the car in gear, says to her, I'm glad you know this is your fault.

Forgetting Maria's instructions, Rob over-waters the ficus tree and the straggly cactus. She paces the length of the loft, her boots thudding on the oiled wooden floor. Weaving in and out past the heavy metal tables piled with tools, stacks of dried blocks of wood, she counts the painted metal thread carriers high up on the ceiling, remnants of the sweatshop the building had been barely fifty years ago. Like a packrat with no judgement she drags broken pallets, a pitted chrome bumper, several three-legged chairs, a box of carpet samples up from the street. Piles them, pairs them, stomps on them, singes them, stares at them. Nothing clicks. Mick badgers her, tells her she needs to produce, to exhibit next year. It's expected, necessary, if she wants to stay ahead of the market.

As her supply of cash dwindles, her consumption of cheap whiskey goes up. She gets thrown out of a couple of neighborhood bars, spends her nights curled up around her stomach pains. Most of her days she walks across the city, counting her steps, trying not to remember. Sometimes the city itself seems to be in cahoots against her. Passing a pawn shop on 42nd Street, a scratchy amplifier blares Sinatra, the one song she needs to forget.

Jonah thumbs through Coach's album covers. how can he like this crap? it's so sappy. he prances with a pretend mic, lip synchs, Fly me to the moon Let me play among the stars Let me see what spring is like, he shouts, on a–Jupiter and Mars. so stupid, he cracks up. why the fuck say A–Jupiter and Mars? she laughs, says quit it. he'll be home soon.

She needs to stay away from mid-town. A few days later, stuck behind a woman with a stroller she runs smack into Mr. and Mrs. Ackroyd. She hears Mrs. telling Mr. to hurry or they'll miss the curtain. Rob tucks her chin, tries to shield her face, takes a drag on her cigarette. They don't notice much less recognize her.

you're a doll Robin, Mrs. Ackroyd says. The kids were? great, Robin says, same as always. she stuffs the three one dollar bills into her pocket. thanks for staying, Mrs. A. says, we didn't realize we'd be out so late. Coach won't worry? nah, she says, smiles to herself as she realizes that she's only about forty dollars shy. a few more months of babysitting jobs and she's got enough. hey, Mr. Ackroyd says, it is pretty late, let me walk you home. I'm good, Mr. Ackroyd, she says. call me Teddy, he says, and I insist, wouldn't want anything to happen on our watch. Robin shrugs, steps out the door. they walk in silence until Teddy says, I've seen you, at night? walking. so? so nothing. it's good to get out of the house. have you ever gone up to the ballfield? away from the street? it's quiet, peaceful. she shakes her head. you haven't? maybe a couple times, she mutters. I heard you're saving for a bike—Jesus Christ! does the whole world know I want a bike? easy, kid. you told my wife I guess. they walk in silence until coming to the through street. so do you want to go up? to the ball-field? I need to get home. I could help you know, with the bike. help how? with the money. for the bike. why would you—Robin stops, takes a step back and looks at Teddy, realizes that it was him, that he was the one who saw her with Danny. that she would be dead if he ever told Coach. he leans over a bit, juts out his chin. you get it, don't you? he says quietly. she whispers, how much? he laughs. that's my girl. what do you need? she sees the number in her head, forty, knows that it's too much, figures if babysitting pays fif-ty cents an hour whatever he wants has to be worth more. seven, she says, seven dollars. he laughs again. you'll go far, kid. the cinderblock walls of the dugout are damp, corrugated plastic roof cracked at the ends. Robin starts to unzip her jeans, slide them down her legs. no, no not that, Teddy says as he sits on the cold, clammy wooden seat. she pulls up her jeans, closes the rivet. what, then? what do you want? unzip my pants. take it out and put it in your mouth. suck it. I never—it's easy. Teddy shows her where to kneel in front of him then takes her head in his hands, one hand on each side of her face. his cock is rising, pushing on the polyester of his sansabelt slacks. she pulls down his zipper, he guides her mouth. she gags, then figures out a better placement. starts to suck, like you would suck on a straw. no, no. he grabs her head again. like this, up and down. up and down. she does as he says and feels him get bigger, harder. he starts moaning, his hands slack on her head. he is like a baby. with just a flick of her tongue, or by speeding up some, slowing down again, she can make him moan more, make him moan louder. or she could bite him, make him scream with pain. her teeth start to close. watch it! she pulls back a bit, resumes the rhythm. he settles against the cinder block wall. his back arches and he spurts into her mouth. she pulls her face away, turns her head and spits. at the bottom of the hill Teddy says, I'll go this way, pointing in the direction of his house. she grabs his arm, what about—he hands her a ten. I don't—keep it, kid. keep the change.

After weeks of prowling the city it happens, of course, in that most clichéd way—when you least expect it, in what we often call the darkest hour before the dawn, but rarely is. The germ of the idea comes while watching a couple of kids play catch in Sara Roosevelt Park. It's not much of a park but the long narrow strip of dirt and grass reminds her of the field she played on, just a few years ago. Every time one kid catches the ball, she feels it, her hands sore and alive, makes her long for it, that moment of complete connection between the passer and receiver.

Jonah stumbles across the field, arms stretched in front of him, head turned back to Coach. as the ball comes near, he opens his arms. the stiff pointed end of the football hits him in the chest, hard enough to knock him backward, then bounces to the ground. for Christ's sake Jonah! Coach yells. how can you be such a moron? catch the damn thing with your hands! use your hands! Jonah bends slowly to pick up the ball, nearly in tears. lemme show you Robin shouts, loud enough for Coach to hear, then under her breath says to Jonah don't whine. just try. please. for once. don't get him started. Jonah stares at her, wipes his nose with his sleeve, lets the ball flop into her hands. he takes a few steps back, sits on the ground, crosses his legs and takes a small pad of paper and a pencil from his jacket pocket. yeah, Coach yells from across the field. draw me a pretty picture. Robin tosses the ball to him, a hard, tight spiral. he catches it, tosses it back in a high arc. see, she say to Jonah as the ball falls into her hands. catch it like this, with your hands, then bring it into your body. Danny comes running up the field. Coach loves Danny. and all his brothers. they're the best players and there are a ton of them, five big boys. strong, terrif-ic athletes, great competitors. he loves them all. Robin likes Danny too. he's the only jock in the smart kids class. they quote Shakespeare to each other, once in a while play catch in the street. he is nice to Jonah, actually spends time with him. Coach yells across the field, three way catch? no, Danny says, a contest. yeah, alright, Robin laughs, first one to drop loses. they set the line of scrimmage at one end of the long dusty field. Robin and Danny play odds/evens. Danny wins. he sets the ball on its point, turns sideways to face his Coach. hike! Coach adjusts the ball, cocks his arm and yells, sidelines. Danny takes off. the ball sails into the air. easily caught. Danny runs back. smirks at Robin. for twenty minutes Coach calls button hooks, sidelines, slants, and the all-time favorite, go long. no drops. the day fades, shadows of the houses at the edge of the field create deep pockets of darkness. can't see a thing, Coach says, time to quit. one more round, Danny says. Robin echoes, somebody has to win. one more round. no drops. just once more, Danny pleads. Robin says, one more and we'll quit. it's Danny's turn. he hikes the ball. Coach yells slant left! Danny takes off, heads into the deepest shadows. the throw is right on the money. his hands reach out. the ball sails through. Danny stares at his hands, at the ball lying a few feet beyond him. crap! I couldn't see it! Danny yells. I could have caught it! really! I just couldn't see it. Coach says, shit, and starts towards him. Robin reaches for him says, my turn, I can win. Coach shakes his head. get off, why'd you fuck with his confidence! I need him to be confident! Danny runs back, I just couldn't see. Coach pats him on the shoulder, son, it's OK. my turn, Robin repeats, my turn. Coach shoves her aside. I said not now! let her have a turn, Danny says, it's the rules. Robin hikes the ball. Coach yells, button hook, his mouth set hard. Robin runs the eight steps straight out, turns and the ball comes flying at her head. she throws her arms up, to protect her face as much as try to catch it. the ball hits her hands with a loud slap. she closes them around it, jams it into her body. the ball sits hard against her chest. it aches and she tries to get a deep breath. I won! she starts to holler but stops dead when she hears Coach turn to Danny saying it's alright, you just couldn't see. she didn't really beat you. Coach puts an arm around Danny, pats him on the shoulder, over and over. Jonah stares at Coach with equal parts hate and hope. Robin watches, her hands stinging, chest throbbing. she got lucky, Coach tells Danny. nah, Danny says. she won. she's good. it doesn't matter, Coach says. she can't be on the team. Wait for me, Coach says to Danny, I'll be right there. Coach snarls at Robin and Jonah, steps close to them and says quietly, go home. take that piece of shit brother of yours and go home. Robin grabs Jonah by his collar, tries to yank him up. you had to start, didn't you, she says. he shrugs her off. shit, Robin says and sits down next to him. show me? he gives her the notebook, a rough sketch of Coach eating a football. she grabs the pencil, laughs as she adds a hand cramming the ball into his mouth. hands are hard to draw, Jonah says in his fake Coach voice. you're pretty good for a girl. she punches him on the arm. can't you just catch the fucking ball? one time? I know you can do it. I know you can. why can't you just catch the ball? Jonah takes back his notebook, helps her to her feet and whispers, I wish it was him. why couldn't it have been him.

After a couple more drinks she thinks about calling Danny. She has thought about it many, many times since she left. Just to hear his voice, talk to, laugh with, someone who knew Jonah, who knew her before she carried those crude carved birds into Mick's gallery. She picks up the phone, says his number out loud, doesn't dial.

too dark to see the baseball. all the other kids gone. hey Puck, Danny asks, you wanna play some more? not baseball she says. you got a football? we could play catch under the lights. nah, he says, walking towards her slowly. he has just turned sixteen, is already tall and broad, needs to shave every other day. they have been friends for years, playing ball with each other, against each other. he reaches her, holds out his arm, taps her lightly on the cheek. slap fight? she laughs. he nods, like we used to. she swings her arm up, knocks his aside and slaps his face. a little harder than he had hit her. he smiles. they trade slaps, neither hitting very hard, faster and faster. he has the advantage. her arms are shorter, she has to stay inside to connect at all. it frustrates her, causes her to hit harder than she means to. he responds, slaps so hard her face is jerked sideways. she hauls off and hits him, as hard as she can, connects with his jaw. he drops his arms. we have to stop, he says quietly. it isn't fair. I'm bigger. I'll always be bigger. and she is astonished that she isn't hitting back, that she is standing there, nearly in tears. she tries to turn away, but he folds his arms around her, pulls her to his chest. they stand in silence, pressing their bodies together. you haven't yet. have you? he says to the top of her head. she feels his hands, one on her back, one on her shoulder, gently rubbing, shakes her head. do you wanna? maybe. yeah. I think. here? he turns their bodies toward the dugout. won't it be cold? she asks. on the chest protector, you can lay on the catcher's chest protector. he sits on the hard wooden bench in the dugout, leans against the cinderblock wall. she straddles him, feet on the bench, knees high to the sides. they kiss softly, harder, with closed eyes. she is amazed by how familiar it feels, not all that different from guarding or blocking, the same push and pull, press and withdraw. the feeling she gets catching a long ball, that joyful moment at the clarity of the connection. he lifts her off his lap, lays her on the damp padded chest protector. she opens her arms as he unbuttons her jeans, then his. it is pitch dark. it is better this way. not seeing each other. she is surprised at her wetness, shocked by the single sharp pain as he enters her, realizes that it is better when she moves, rocks her hips. it doesn't take long. he withdraws just as he comes, spraying her shirt. he lies next to her, on the cold concrete, propped on one elbow. here, he says, licking his fingers, reaching down. he rubs her. she is in awe. she has never felt this, for a brief second wonders how he knows to do this, then she explodes with a short, hard shout that turns into laughter. yeah, he says quietly. I knew you'd get it. when he stands, fully dressed, he says, about Debbie, you know. so I can't. you and me. we can't. yeah I know, she says. you're going steady. and Coach, he says. Coach would have a fit. she catches her breath, nearly cries again, blurts out, has Debbie been up here? he laughs. you're the only one I would bring up here. what the fuck does that mean? not like that! you're the only one I know who would get it. why it's OK. you get it. get what? that it's ok to just do it. not always make it some big thing, some "do you love me" thing, till death do us part thing. it's about feeling good. making each other feel good.

you're my friend Robin, not just some girlfriend. only you. you get it. that this is just another way to play.

She puts down the receiver then lugs all the rusty metal, useless chairs to the far end of the loft next to the dying plants, stacks the pallets next to the stove. Positioning a block of wood on a work table, she grabs a chisel, a hammer, lights a cigarette, murmurs, You're right, Julius, Cowards do die yadda yadda yadda. Time to be valiant.

Mick nods, over and over, as he walks across the floor of Rob's studio. Oh yeah, yeah, yeah he says softly. This is good. Good. Good.

Carved from the left over pier pilings she had assembled for *Disfigure,* this piece is about four feet tall, two feet wide, only about a foot deep and hangs flat on the wall. There are two hands, a little bigger than life-size, thrusting forward from the rough-hewn slab that suggests a torso, shoulders and arms. The roughness of the arms morphs into well-formed wrists. But the hands are exquisitely carved, fully realized, fingers perfectly formed, knuckles deeply lined, well-defined cuticles and nails. The hands are cupped, facing each other, about ten inches apart, the left slightly higher than the right. There is a great tension between them, a space longing to be filled.

So ok? she says, exhaling a cloud of smoke.

Make more. You'll be the season opener again, late September.

Will do, she says. She gestures to the back of the loft. You wanna stay for a while?

Your Grace won't be coming?

She's not mine! I see her at her place uptown. Besides, you're the one who told me to be nice to her!

There's nice and there's—

Jesus, Mick. Don't make it so complicated. Do you wanna fuck or not.

He lays his palm on the small of her back, pushes her toward the bed, How can I turn down such a genteel offer.

Rob points out the gallery window and whispers to Mick, What the hell is he doing here?

That's Geoffrey Stevenson—

I know who it is! What's he doing here?

I invited him.

For what?

He loved *Disfigure*. I want him to talk to you—

No!

He'll write a preview for the opening. Did you come up with a title?

She shakes her head.

If we get lucky he'll do an article afterward. Just a few questions—

I don't know how talk about it!

Just follow my lead. Have I ever done anything to hurt you?

Other than sleep with half of the women in Manhattan? she thinks. As Stevenson enters the gallery Rob wonders, Why is this guy such a big deal?

If you didn't know Geoffrey Stevenson you would never guess he is who he is. His position in the NY art scene is unique. No one else wields the kind of power he has over artist's lives, the success or failure of galleries. But he doesn't look the part, even a little. His stomach strains the buttons of his wrinkled shirt, the pathetic attempt of his combover, his straggly beard, all scream over-the-hill college professor. Standing side by side with Mick—slim, trim, his curly hair perfectly messy,

very much at ease in his tight jeans and black T shirt—
Stevenson looks like somebody knocking on the door at
dinner time selling magazine subscriptions.

As Mick leads Stevenson to her work hanging on the
walls, Rob sits on a stool behind the counter aching for
invisibility. Stevenson stands still, rocking a little on his
heels, shaking his head side to side, murmuring to himself.

Same wood?

Mick nods. Yes, the pier pilings she's collected.

Why the same materials?

Rob? He asked—

I heard! I like it, she says to Stevenson from across the
room. I like the wood. It's still hard. You have to work it.
To herself she says, And because it's fucking free.

Come on over here, he says with a smile. I won't bite.

Rob slides off the stool, crosses the room saying under her breath, Yeah but I might.

You didn't leave any of the creosote visible this time,
Stevenson says. Why?

Rob shrugs, looks at Mick. He prompts her with his
chin.

I don't know, she says sullenly. They needed to be
clean. I didn't want them to seem dirty. Or to smell.

He grunts. You know, he says, moving closer to her,
they remind me of some of Camille Claudel's work, that
movement from rough to realized.

Mick nods, says, Great reference. You've seen her
work, haven't you?

Rob backs away, smiles blankly, Yeah, I've seen that. Of course.

Stevenson reaches for one of the carved hands, follows the line of it in the air. Show title is still undecided?

We're working on it, Mick says.

I can write this up. I'll need the title.

Mick nods, looking pointedly at Rob.

She shrugs.

Will there be any viewer participation in—

No! Rob says quickly. They are what they are.

And what is that, Stevenson asks.

Hands!

Yes, of course, Stevenson says. But what do they mean? Are they supposed to convey desire? Hope? The belief that emptiness is our constant state? That our hands will never be filled?

What do they mean? Rob says over her shoulder as she walks into the back room, comes out with an empty wine bottle. She yells, Think fast! and under-hands it in a tight spiral right to Stevenson. He puts his hands up, way too late, and the bottle goes through them, hits him in the chest, falls to the floor. A dribble of sour white wine sprinkles his shoes.

As Rob heads out the door she says, Name of the show? *Catch*.

Mick sits on the edge of Rob's bed, ties his shoes, stands, zips his pants.

She leans near the window in a pool of bleak light

shining through the dirty glass, slams her coffee cup down on the wide sill. Come on! she hollers. You gotta be kidding me!

Jesus, Robbie, don't yell at me. And don't blame me. It's the only job I could find for you.

Why can't I work the counter at Gem Spa again?

They did me a favor, taking you when you had no papers. But you blew it. Nobody wants to deal with you. Why did you have to be such a bitch?

They were morons, wouldn't listen—

Not gonna happen.

What about the new work?

I only sold two. It's not hitting like the first stuff.

Why the hell not? It the same wood, the same style—

You fucked it up with that stunt with Stevenson. Not getting reviewed killed sales. Christ only knows what he said to people. Buyers need to be told what to like. I know the hands are good. Even he liked them. But it's not going to be easy. I'm gonna have to work it, work harder to get them sold.

So you want me to paint sofa-sized oils? To sell at some Howard Johnsons?

Mick laughs, Worse. The BayView Motel. In Queens.

I'm not going to fucking Queens. Queens is a small New Jersey.

You can paint right here. They'll pick them up. Look. It's a no-brainer. Just paint from the picture they give you. Flowers, landscapes, pretty cottages. Yeah it's schlock. But it's schlock you get paid for. You don't have to meet buyers, you don't have to meet anybody. You don't even sign them. Nobody will know.

Do you see any oil paints around here?

They want you to use acrylic. Dries faster.

Come on, Mick. I'm not a painter!

Mick waves his cigarette, dismissing her.

No, really! I mean it, I am a lousy painter!

I showed them copies of your drawings. You'll be fine.

I didn't do...haven't done that stuff in years.

The money is decent. Go buy some paint—the Golden brand, it's better than Liquitex. Stop at the gallery and pick up the photo and canvas. And for Christ's sake, stop whining.

For several days Rob tries to reproduce the grassy path lined with pink flowers and tall bushes that leads by the quaint cottage with smoke coming out of the crooked chimney. The proportions are working, the composition is fine, but it's the colors that are killing her. She squeezes paint from tubes, mixes, mixes and mixes again, looking for the specific green of the grass, the grey-blue of the coming twilight in the picture.

At the point she is ready to stick her knife in the canvas, she pulls a duffel bag from the back of a closet. The padlock that she forced through the grommets is stiff, slightly rusted. She turns the key carefully, worried it might snap off. She slowly un-pleats the top of the duffel then pulls out the contents, setting the papers, the books, on the bed. The last thing is a small portfolio. No one has seen this, not even Mick. She unzips it, lays it open on her work table. Her hands are stiff and dry as she sorts the papers, finds the color wheel, the studies Jonah did in high school. She doesn't intend to look at the rest but finds herself taking out the drawings, the notebook, the creased envelope of photographs. She had added one, before she fled—a Polaroid of Jonah at the kitchen table, probably twelve years old, probably close to the only night he asked to walk with her.

the night is black, no moon, no stars. the bluish-white light from TV sets flicker in the windows, the same color as their breath in the cold. the streets are deserted, the suburban neighborhood silent. nobody sees him for real, Jonah says. nobody asks. they like him! Robin yells. best coach they ever had! she points to one house. but she did, Mrs. Cassidy. she asked. once. Danny's mother? he grabs her sleeve. what did you tell her? what did you say? she yanks her arm away. what could I say? they LIKE the way he is! he wins, he's a winner. she pushes him hard. he stumbles, says, don't get mad at me! I'm not mad, she mutters. yeah, he says. I get it. it's like it's contagious. they walk in the cold, around and around the small neighborhood. he asks, so this is what you do? just walk around? it helps. does it? some. you? she asks, do you do anything? back in his room he slides a black case, about the size of a big magazine, out from under his mattress, unzips it, opens it wide on the bed. he sets aside a pile of studies, class work, to reveal the portraits. she gasps. drawing after drawing, all in black and white—pencil or charcoal. it was her. you could feel her, more than just look at her. she expected them to start talking. she asks him, how can you do this? you were just a little kid. he reaches inside a volume of The World Book and pulls out a creased envelope, holds it out. three black and white photos. of their mother. where? she whispers, how? he says, looking for rope in the basement. he missed them. she holds the photos like they will evaporate if she breathes on them. all I remember is her smell, he says. from the bubble baths, she says. she took them on Mondays, after he left. Jonah gestures to the pile of drawings. keep looking, look at everything. at the bottom of the pile is a large spiral-bound notebook. she opens it slowly. pictures, like comic book drawings. in color. violent, screaming color. Jonah stabbing Coach, blood spurting from his stomach. Jonah strangling Coach, his eyes bugging out. Jonah running Coach over with a car. you asked, he says, asked what I did. this is what I do. the front door opens, Coach's keys land on the kitchen table with a bang. Jonah's hands shake as he grabs the notebook and the drawings, slides them into the portfolio, zips it and shoves it under his mattress. he tucks the photos back into The World Book, puts his hands in his pockets, sits down on the bed rocking back and forth. she goes to feed Coach.

The phone wakes Rob from a sound sleep. Who?

Amanda Patterson.

Yeah?

From Chic Decor. For the painting.

Already?

Today is the deadline.

Oh. Wow. I'll drop the key down in a coffee can. Wait by the front door.

Climbing five flights isn't in my job description, Amanda says. You bring it. And soon. We've got a van here and a bunch more pick-ups.

Alright alright. Be right down. Exit, she mutters, pursued by a bear.

She takes one more look at the sofa-sized oil, tests a corner and sees that it's still just a tad wet. She takes a deep breath and heads out the door. Careful not to bang it on the dirty staircase, she sees the woman and a guy standing beside a rental van. The woman wears an off-white pants suit, high heels. Her dyed blonde hair is a not-so-bouncy attempt at a Farrah Fawcett. The man, slightly balding, has on a blue uniform, like a janitor.

You didn't pack it? Amanda says. Didn't even wrap it?

It's still—Nobody told me—

You call yourself an artist? You're supposed to know things like that. Don't put it on the sidewalk! she yells. Jesse, open the back.

Jesse opens the back of the van, says Here, set it on this blanket.

When do I get paid?

The contract is with Mick Taylor. We pay him. But I need to compare it.

To what?

This. Amanda fishes in her oversized purse, pulls out a wrinkled color xerox of the photo Rob has been working from, holds it up against the painting. No, no, no, she says, shaking her head. It's off. The customer won't like this. I'm not liking this.

Rob steps toward the van door. Not liking what?

Nah, nah, nah, Amanda goes on. I'm not taking this.

Rob steps closer to her. Why not?

Look, she holds out the xerox. It's not right. The color is off.

Rob takes the copy. That's not what I had to work from! The photo is different.

Amanda just shakes her head.

I'll get the photo, Rob says. Just wait. I'll show you. This is different.

Forget it, Amanda says. Jesse, give the painting back. We've got to get going.

Jesse takes the painting from the van, tries to hand it to Rob.

No! Rob shrieks, pushes it back to him. I did it right! You have to pay me.

Get out of our way, Amanda shrieks back.

Jesse, only the driver of this operation, is confused. He lets go of the piece. Rob falls forward into him, the painting goes sideways, landing square against Amanda's chest. The greens and grey-blues Rob had taken such pains to carefully mix spread a snot-like smear on Amanda's chest.

Are you kidding me! Amanda hollers.

He let go! It's not my fault—

Jesse! Get in the van. We're outta here.

Rob stands on the sidewalk, the smeared painting hanging half off the curb in a puddle of grease. You have to pay me!

Jesse closes the back door, gets in the driver's seat, starts the engine.

Rob's heart is racing, blood pounding in her ears. She picks up a broken brick from the gutter, runs behind the van, yelling, I did it right! You have to pay! as she slams the brick through the van's back window.

Jesus, Robbie, Mick says, what the hell did you do?

It wasn't my fault! It looked like the photo. I know it did!

I can't get you out of this.

She holds the summons in her hands, stares at it. I have to go to court?

They are pressing charges.

For what?

You broke the window with a brick!

I didn't mean to! I just meant to hit the van.

And that's better how? He takes the summons from her. But the big thing is the assault charge.

Assault? What assault?

If this wasn't so serious it would be funny. She says you attacked her with a painting.

For Christ's sake! She was being a jerk. I was just being a jerk back.

You could go to jail!

For being a jerk?

Mick shakes his head. It's not normal, Rob. Your definition of a jerk is not normal.

She sinks down on the battered couch, the cramping grinding in her guts causes her to shiver. Can you help me? she whispers.

Why don't you call your upper west side girlfriend?

Hey can we focus on what's important here? She looks up at him with that same look she had on her face the first day she walked into his gallery. Desperate, defiant need.

I've got a lawyer. I'll ask David.

When Rob meets Mick she is wearing a black skirt, white blouse and back flats under her army surplus jacket.

Maybe take off the jacket, he says.

I feel like a waitress, she says as they ride the elevator to David's mid-town office.

Are you ever going to get a normal coat? Just fold that thing over your arm. And play the game, watch your mouth. Don't embarrass me.

Rob is floored. And embarrassed. He's never spoken to her like this. She had no idea she has the ability to embarrass him.

They wait for twenty minutes, then are ushered into a small office, file cabinets lining one wall, bookshelves on the other. There is a wide window, nearly floor-to-ceiling behind the lawyer's desk. Pigeons have taken over the sill, stalking each other, pecking at nothing. David stands, shakes hands with Mick, motions to the two chairs across from his desk.

It could be worse, David says.

Like the guillotine instead of the chair? Rob says.

Mick elbows her.

You're lucky, Rob. The courts have these new programs, diversion programs, to keep first offenders out of prison.

If I was really lucky, she would have let me show her the photo—

Mick gives her the side eye, asks David, What about damages?

They are asking for ten thousand, but I can get that cut in half.

Rob leans forward. Five thousand DOLLARS? Five THOUSAND dollars? What the fuck for?

Mick puts his hand on her arm, presses her back into her seat.

Damage to the van, to the paintings in the van, to the clothes Amanda Patterson was wearing.

I just saw a white pants suit at the Goodwill for seven bucks! I don't have five thousand dollars!

Shut up! Mick says through clenched teeth. Sit down and shut up. He turns to David. Are you sure you can get it down to five?

David nods.

And your fee?

David leans over his desk, says to Rob, We can take it out in trade.

Rob starts, stares at him. Trade what?

David smiles, I want one of those hand things.

Her eyes narrow, then widen. You mean my sculpture?

David nods, Yeah, what else? He says to Mick, You'll be at the Met opening Friday?

Wouldn't miss it.

My sister is in town. I want you to meet her.

Hey! Rob butts in. So what the fuck do I do? To get diverted?

David laughs, hands her some papers. You have to complete an Anger Management Course, run by the City. Six two-hour classes, one a week for six weeks. Will start in early January. If you pass and receive a certificate, there will be nothing on your record. If you fail you will go to jail for five to eight months.

Rob takes the papers, scans them, says, I can do this. Where is the course?

David points to the address on the envelope. In Jamaica.

Like the island?

No like Queens.

For the first time in a week, Mick smiles.

The building would make one hell of a bunker. Squat, square, white-painted brick, tiny slit windows, a product of urban renewal. Barely twenty years old, the center has been closed due to budget cuts, re-opened when crime spiked, closed, re-opened, over and over, more times than anybody wants to remember. When something breaks, it stays that way – no working locks on bathroom stalls, linoleum peeling, ceiling tiles water-stained, basketball hoops without nets, every third light bulb burned out. It is barely ever cleaned, no attempt made to discover the source of the obvious mold. Some clever kid spray-painted a letter on the sign on the outside wall. Repeated attempts to remove it has only made it more visible. The Malcolm T. Giddens WRecreation Center doesn't promise a thing.

Kathleen Morrison, a greying social worker, once tall, is now a little stooped from carrying the post-menopausal ten. A mother/child relations specialist, she is sure she is not the right person to be running this new treatment modality. Anger management to keep offenders out of jail? But she's so close to the end. All she wants is to get through the modules so she can issue the certificate that states they successfully completed the course. This is the third group she has run and at the end of this one, a mere six weeks away, she will age-out and receive her slightly-less-than-hoped-for pension.

Tonight's group is small, only four, supposed to have been five, two men and three women, but one of the men was violated two days ago. Kathleen sits in the Rec Center office fronted with a chicken-wire glass window, hidden behind faded, torn notices reading Rec League Cancelled and No Smoking. She watches as they come in, a thick manila folder on the desk in front of her detailing their crimes, the class list paper-clipped to the front. More out of control people, she says to herself, just what I need.

At 6:45 the first to arrive is a very stylish black woman. From her file Kathleen knows she is over fifty but she looks a whole lot closer to thirty, highly manicured and dressed in a yellow pants suit, definitely by some designer. She sniffs the air, wrinkles her nose, holds her arms close to her sides. Vanessa Thompson. At about five to seven in comes two of them, a white male and female. He holds the door for her, she motions for him to go first, he scowls, shrugs, then lets go of the door. He is in his mid-thirties wearing a grey sweatshirt stretched tight over the beginnings of a paunch, clean but baggy jeans, definitely growing out his mullet. Damon Sykes. He peers in the gym, grunts, scowls again and walks on. The woman is Nadine Littleton, thirty-something, curly blonde hair, one of those long-limbed androgynous looking women, black boots, worn jeans, a red tee under her unbuttoned denim shirt. She turns back to the closing door for a second, shakes her head and proceeds up the hall to the classroom.

Time's up, Kathleen says to herself. As she comes out

of the office, the front door is flung open and a woman rushes into the building.

Is this it? she asks Kathleen, panting.

Is this what? Kathleen answers, knowing it is Robin Morgan.

The place for the class. The anger class.

The one you are supposed to be on time for?

I'm here! The fucking subway. Queens! I got fucking lost.

Language! Kathleen barks.

Sorry! Rob barks back.

Follow me.

Vanessa, Nadine and Damon are scattered around the room, sitting at the battered blonde Formica desk/chair assemblies. Rob sits at the desk closest to the door. Kathleen collects each person's form that indicates yes, this is the person mandated to Anger Management. She carefully compares the name on the form with each person's photo ID, then ticks off each on the class list. She slides the forms into the file she has placed on the large table at the front of the class.

Yes, good, she says briskly. I am Mrs. Morrison. She looks directly at Rob, Being on time is one of the requirements to pass this course. Any further lateness will result in dismissal from the program. Now please, move down to the front row, here.

Do we have to? Damon asks.

Yes.

But I'm left handed, Damon whines. There's no left-hand desk there. That's why I took that one.

So bring that one up, Rob says. Don't be a moron.

Who the hell are you? Damon says to Rob.

Just come up to the front, Kathleen says, all of you.

Damon drags the desk noisily.

Kathleen picks up her stiff, barely used manual, opens it to the first page and page and reads aloud:

We are all aware that anger is a powerful emotion. We are here to understand it and learn to deal with it. Most people do not know what to do with anger other than explode or repress it. Over the next six weeks you will learn how to identify what triggers your anger and how to deal with it. It is very important that you know that you there will always be times when you get angry. Life is full of frustration, pain, and you can't control the actions of others. The only thing you can change is how you react and not let your anger control you.

Sounds like the beginning of a twelve step, Damon mutters.

A thing you know something about? Rob says, loud enough for him to hear.

Kathleen hands out the manuals. For this first class we begin with Exercise One on page six. Take all the time you need. You don't need to finish today, but pay attention to the instructions.

Introduce Yourself

You will succeed in this course if you are able to admit

Rob pulls her sketchbook out of her bag, chews on the end of her pen, thinks, Shit. I don't have a problem with anger, I have a problem with stupid people that make me angry. But I gotta get this right. What do they want from me? Don't shy away from memories it says. Examine my life. Be thorough it says. Honest.

She holds up her hand. Mrs. Morrison? Who is gonna read this?

I have no idea, Kathleen says to herself. She smiles her best fake smile and says, Just think of it as a diary.

Rob smiles a fake smile back but thinks, Why not.

It was so ugly, where he took us. If you had to pick a song to describe it the only song that would fit is the one by that craggy-voiced Malvina Reynolds. Put her in front of a pile of warped 2x4s singing Little Boxes. A suburb. As ticky-tacky as it could be. Seventy-two houses on three looped streets, the closest town more than three miles away. By highway. You couldn't walk there. You couldn't walk anywhere. The streets had stupid names—JoLynn Lane, Sally Way, Diane Court. Stumps of big trees all over the place, thorny bushes and skimpy pine trees. Every house exactly the same. Architectural disasters, split-levels. It looked like there was a small house sunk half-way in the dirt, bottoms of the windows touching the ground, with a bigger house stuck on top. Three choices—off-white, puke-beige or gun-metal grey. We ended up at one of the bends of the middle loop, a curved lot with a fat pie-shaped front lawn and a tiny backyard. Our house, a grey one, sat diagonally across the lot, closer to the street, like it wanted to escape. We arrived late at night. The white post stuck at the end of the driveway had a black mailbox with a red number on it. In the full moon the shadow of the mailbox spread out across the street, like a skinny, dead animal.

I was ten and Jonah was six when we left New York. Coach hated the city, complained all the time. I don't know what the big deal was. He wasn't there much. Traveled from Monday morning until Friday night. Selling sports equipment. But after she died we up and left. He sold our house, the house that was her mother's, the house she loved, filled with things she picked out—cheap stuff from the Goodwill, things we found on the street. She would see it and have to have it. Especially lamps, said she needed more light in her life. We had a ton of them. Way more than there were outlets for. We could have lit up every room in every house on the block. And chairs. She loved those wing back chairs, said it was like sitting on the lap of an angel. We left all the lights and all the chairs. Every single one. Hell, except for beds and kitchen stuff, we left most everything else. I threw a monster tantrum and made him take a small end-table, blonde oak with a green leather inset on the top that had a row of gold rectangles printed along the edges of the leather. I would sit on the table and she would tie my shoes. I knew how to tie my own shoes from when I was like three years old, but we did this, every day, before I went to school. She'd bend to my feet, I could smell Dial soap, feel her un-brushed long dark hair tickle my cheeks. Most days she got distracted, had to go check that the stove was off, make sure the water wasn't running, the back window locked. While she was gone I pressed my palms into the sharp corners, counted the rectangles until she came back. She always came back.

He threw out the pictures. Photos of her and him. Photos of me with her, of Jonah with her. Told us not to talk about her. All we could say was that our mother died. In an accident. She came out of the subway at 59th and Lex, got turned around, stepped off the curb and got hit by a bus.

We went to the first place he got a job, teaching Phys Ed and coaching football at a nowhereville high school. We were the new kids but it didn't really matter. Nobody knew anybody because everybody was from someplace else. The place wasn't even a real place. There was nothing here before these houses. Nobody could have come from here.

I learned to shut up and pretend I didn't hate the no subway, no corner store, no library, no sidewalk, middle of fucking nowhere we ended up. Instead I counted stuff. In my head. Counted my steps, counted the cracks in the pavement, the number of mailboxes I passed. I kept it inside, like a volcano, churning but not erupting with boiling hot lava, enough to bury the sub-division we lived in, enough to bury the whole stinking world. It gave me ulcers. Really. At fourteen years old I collapsed on the street in front of our house. Jonah had to call an ambulance. The doctor was surprised, thought I was faking it. How could a teen-ager have ulcers? A genetic disposition, he told them. Their mother had ulcers from a young age too.

We rode a bus to school, a stupid yellow and black bus. It wasn't easy for me. Busses, as you can imagine, were not my favorite things. The driver was this nasty woman, long grey hair coiled up on her head like a pile of dirty snow. She never talked. She yelled. Get on! Sit down! Shut up! Get off! When I couldn't stand it anymore I yelled back at her and she would stop the bus, just stop it in the middle of the road, get up from the driver's seat, turn and stare. Cars backed up, horns honking, and she stared daggers at me until I sat down and shut up. Everybody hated me for it. But because I was Coach's daughter and my mother had died nobody was allowed to get mad at me. At least they couldn't show it. I got away with a lot of shit for a while. Except with Coach. He said I was a moron, to stop being so sensitive, that even my little brother could ride the bus. For Christ's sake forget about it, get on the fucking thing, sit down and shut up.

It's us against the world, he told us. Over and over. Just us against them now. He made a plan, said the only way we were going to make it was if we followed the plan. He put a chart outside the bathroom door with time slots for showers, a bigger chart on the fridge with different colored blocks saying who did what when. There was only me and Jonah and he was still really little so who was he kidding? Who the hell else was gonna do everything. Garbage was green, Toilets blue, Vacuuming yellow and Laundry white. He got a step ladder so I could reach the washer dials. A suction cup with a pencil tied to a string was next to the chart. To check off the job when it was done.

It took months but we finally ran out of casseroles. Every mother in the neighborhood came by with a casserole when we moved in. Tuna surprise, baked spaghetti, chicken and rice in mushroom soup. We ditched the ones with jello, didn't even bother to freeze them, one of the few things Coach and I ever agreed on. And he met them at the door. Nobody came in our house and we didn't go into anybody else's. Our business was our business, he said, we were fine just how we were, didn't need anybody else. He put a blackboard in the rec room next to the kitchen with the menus for the week and once the freezer emptied out I had to cook. I stood on a kitchen chair. It was hit or miss for a while, but the meals were simple. I got pretty good pretty quick. I could check the spaghetti or potatoes to see if they were done but not the steak, he hated it if I cut into it. The timer on the oven was way at the top so I used the Quality of Mercy speech. My mother took me to see The Merchant for my ninth birthday, not too long before she was gone. I would heat the broiler really hot, lay in the steak, say the speech in my head, two times all the way through the whole thing, flip it over, say it once more and it ended rare and bloody, just like he liked it. Hamburgers in a frying pan took three times through that speech in Richard the Third from Now is the winter of our discontent to the lascivious playing of the lute. Salad was exactly the same every night, lettuce, cucumber, tomato with Italian dressing. Didn't need any timing. Even though he wasn't home much, the menu was the menu. He would check to make sure I had used the ingredients. One time I wasn't paying attention, forgot what he was like, and got fancy, cut the carrots for beef stew into a flower shape. He stuck one on the end of his fork, said What the hell is this? Where did you learn this? It's pretty, Jonah said, like artwork. I didn't ask you. My hands started shaking as I ladled stew into my bowl. It's nothing, I muttered. Speak up! I like carving, I whispered. I watched her once. She did that to the carrots. And she cut herself, didn't she! I shrugged. Didn't she! I don't remember that. He pushed away from the table, said as he walked out the door, What, you think you're some kind of artist? Just chop the fucking vegetables like a normal person.

It was better when he wasn't there. Jonah and I ate together every night, I did the dishes, he dried and we checked off the boxes. I forgot sometimes. Not to do the job, but to check it off. Most times the punishment was drop and give me twenty. Push-ups. I could do twenty push-ups. No problem. But Jonah, it usually took the poor kid five minutes to even get up to ten. Coach would get disgusted or bored, call him a moron, roll him over with his foot onto his back and walk away. But sometimes, if his team lost or— we never knew why, why it would happen, when it might happen. We didn't even know him, he wasn't around much before she died. But sometimes when we messed up he would sneer at us, shake his head, point to the kitchen chairs, snarl at us to sit down. He yanked the pencil off the fridge, sat across from us, laid the pencil carefully on the table between us and just stared at it. Jonah's leg would start shaking,

I clenched my teeth, gripped the edge of the table. He would make a fist with his right hand, hold it up to shoulder height, look me in the eye, then slam that fist down on the table. The pencil jumped, Jonah ducked his head, I bit my tongue. Then he would breathe out, one huge blast of air and say, How could I have produced such complete morons. Use the fucking pencil!

We kept to ourselves, me and Jonah. I walked him to his bus, waited for mine. Walked right home. Nobody bothered with us. But once he became the winningest coach in the history of the world everybody wanted to be my friend, everybody said they wanted to help us out. People brought pies at Thanksgiving, cookies at Christmas. Steaks for summer cookouts. All met at the door, nobody inside the house. He had a name but nobody used it, not even us. He was Coach. Jonah drew a terrific cartoon of him as a Wells Fargo Stage Coach, red faced, hollering behind horses huffing and puffing to get the ball over the goal line. It was a riot. Coach didn't think so. The only things Coach found funny were the drill sergeant on Gomer Pyle and the dumb one on Car 54 Where Are You.

School was mostly boring but it was at least better than being at home. Once Jonah and I got in the same school I spent a lot of time making sure he wasn't getting picked on. He just couldn't keep his mouth shut, correcting everybody, asking question after question, drove even me crazy sometimes. A typical conversation with Jonah would begin with him saying Did you know that when the dinosaurs got killed by the meteor that the tidal wave was a mile high? Wow, that must have been something. Why is a mile 5,280 feet, it's stupid. Why not 5200 or 5300? I don't know. Do you think you would die by drowning. When? When the mile high tidal wave came, what else? How would I know? You'd probably get hit with a tree or a building first, so it wouldn't be drowning, it would be quick. I had one friend, Danny, we did stuff together once in a while, play catch, listen to music. And he was the only one to give Jonah the time of day. I would watch them, Danny listening patiently while Jonah carefully explained that Batman was better than Superman because Batman didn't have any super powers but he protected a whole city while Superman could just hit the bad guys and fly away. But mostly being in my family was like being in the army. Or in jail. Every minute of the day mapped out, up on some list. It's not like what you think about when somebody says they had a crappy childhood. We didn't get beat up all the time, or starved. But you could never tell what might push him over the edge, when he was going to blow. The times when nothing happened, those were the worst. No way to relax. You had to keep watching for it, waiting.

Each week when I did the grocery shopping I waited until his car pulled out of the Shop Rite parking lot before going up the sidewalk at the strip mall to make sure this bike was still in the window. Glossy black frame, gleaming chrome handlebars and pedals. The same sign hanging from the ceiling in thick black letters, $49.95, plus tax. I figured it out. It came to a total of $52.40. Coach said I could have it if I paid for it myself. He gave me fifty dollars and a list each Saturday morning, food money for the week. Back in my room, in my bottom desk drawer was $11.05. I had saved it by finding sales on stuff on the list. It took seven months. I wasn't stealing. Not exactly. It was like my mother used to tell me when she sent me to the corner store for milk. Get yourself a pretzel with the change, she always said. Maybe two. So instead of pretzels, I kept the change. But at this rate, I would be ancient before I had enough. I needed $41.35 more.

My first idea was a total failure. A paper route. Just in our neighborhood. I finally got Coach to say yes, that I'd get up at five, meet the guy out by the highway and fold the papers myself. That I would be back in time to make his breakfast at 6:30. I called the number for the Raritan Gazette and the guy on the phone laughed at me. You sound like a girl, he bellowed. Are you? A girl? It's called a paper BOY. Do you know how much these papers weigh? I can do it, I said. I'm strong. And fast. Yeah, right and as soon as you get a boyfriend—- I just turned thirteen, I yelled, why the hell would I want a boyfriend? Watch your language, he said. Please, I could really use the money. What's your name? And I hung up. If I told him my name he would know I was Coach's daughter and there would be hell to pay because I said I needed money. Then I got lucky. One Friday night Mrs. Ackroyd from up the block knocked on our door. First time ever. It seemed her regular babysitter got sick and she needed someone to watch her two kids Saturday night.

You're a little young but I know you're good with your brother, she said. I've watched you. Your dad isn't home much. Everything OK? She tried to see past my shoulder, into the living room. Do you need any help? I closed the door half-way, leaned on the frame, tried to, but couldn't look her in the eye. We don't need help, I blurted. Hey, what you're asking. Is this a job? With pay?

She laughed, Of course. I'll pay you what I pay all our babysitters. Fifty cents an hour. We should be gone from six to about ten. I will give them dinner. All you have to do is watch TV and put them to bed.

Four hours, two dollars. For watching Flipper with some little kids. I didn't even know babysitting was a thing. All I'd need was more jobs like this and I'd be riding my bike down the highway into town, into a whole new world.

Miracle of miracles, Coach said yes, babysit all you want, as long as you do your work. It didn't take long, I got the money together quicker than I thought I would. But, surprise, surprise, he ripped the ground out from under me. Like usual, he dropped me off at the Shop Rite and I headed straight to the strip mall. When he came back for me, he could take the groceries and I would ride my bike. Free, at least for the three miles to our house. And I would have it, would be able to ride outside our stupid neighborhood. But it wasn't there. There was no bike in the window. I ran into the store, yelled, Where is it? This bald guy in chinos and a denim shirt came out from behind the counter. What are you yelling about, where is what? That bike, the one that was in the window! He shrugged, it's gone. Gone where, how? Well it didn't drive itself off. I sold it the other day. You couldn't, it was mine! Calm down, I have another one. He went to a back room, wheeled out a pink-framed bike with a yellow seat. Same model, he said, the girl's version. That's NOT the same! I want the black one, with the cross bar! I would have to order it, he said, could take a few weeks. I NEED it now! Don't be so dramatic, how can you NEED a bike? Tell me who bought it, I said, maybe I can buy it from them. Coach Morgan bought it, he said it was for one of his players, most Improved Performance Award.

I never did get a bike, but I stashed the cash in a coffee can in the basement. He never went in the basement.

Life got better when I got into high school. They put me in the smart class so at least I wasn't bored. And I got to see Danny more. He was really smart for a jock. He was my Chem Lab partner, sat next to me on class trips. Did Shakespeare scenes with me, like I used to do with my mother. Once in a while, even though he was on the school team, we would play catch in the street, or up at the ballfield. I did well in school but I could have failed every subject and Coach wouldn't have noticed. He signed my report card with all As and Jonah's with Cs in everything except Art with the same pen and same look on his face. We were not on the team, were never gonna be on the team.

Rob arrives twenty minutes early for the second class. She waits on the concrete bench outside the rec center, strikes a match to light a cigarette.

that is so good! her mother smiles, you'll get the Free Art Lessons for sure! the Draw Me matchbook cover, now empty of matches, is opened flat on the kitchen table next to Rob's copy of the confederate soldier printed on the back. now do the one on the front, her mother says, the woman's face, it's harder. what about mine? Jonah asks, pushing a drawing across the table. a perfect blue crayon rendering of the woman's face, complete with shading and hatching. wow, her mother says, you don't even NEED art lessons! I can do it too, Robin says, grabbing the crayon out of Jonah's hand. it's good, it's ok, her mother says, you can both be artists.

Rob? Nadine pokes her on the shoulder. Earth to Rob!
She looks up, looks around. Crap! Am I late?
Almost.
Thank you all for arriving on time, Kathleen says, nodding to Rob and Nadine. Before we begin today's work we all have to agree that we will follow the conditions and rules for these sessions. She turns to a blackboard. First are the four conditions you must meet to successfully complete the course and receive your cer-

tificate. You already know the first one. As she points to each, she reads out loud:

Be on time for every session
Remain for the entire session
Participate in the discussion
Hand in homework in a timely fashion.

Homework? Damon mutters. What are we, ten years old?

Vanessa raises her hand, What if we get sick?

Kathleen sighs, thinking Always, always somebody. You will need to submit a doctor's note with a valid excuse and you will have to make up the session.

She points to a second list. Here are the rules, First is that we have only One conversation at a time. No side comments, no off-topic conversations. Next is No interrupting. If you want to make a comment, wait for the person speaking to finish. Third is Treat each other with respect—no eye rolling, laughing at others, talking behind backs, pejorative remarks.

Next is Actively...

What's that? Vanessa asks. Pejorative.

She interrupted, Rob says.

Kathleen ignores her. Pejorative means...

It's being deliberately mean, Nadine explains, saying nasty things about someone.

Now she interrupted, Damon smirks.

Next rule, Kathleen says, is Actively listen to each other. Active listening is not making assumptions but sincerely listening to what is being said before you make up your mind.

Fat chance, Damon mutters.

Rob says, Does that count as a side comment?

Nadine laughs, I'd say yes but that would be a side comment on a side comment.

And the last rule, Kathleen says loudly, maybe the most important one is we play by Vegas rules.

What? Vanessa asks. She had not been actively listening.

It means, Rob says, that what we do in here stays in here.

I'd put odds on that, Nadine says.

Good one, Rob laughs.

Rob, Kathleen says, If you would let me...

Hey, I'm just participating.

Ignoring her again, Kathleen says, What people say in these sessions needs to be treated with respect. We need to trust each other so we can have honest conversations.

There's that honest thing again, Damon mutters. Trust, my ass.

Rob holds up her hand.

What? Kathleen asks, a little sharper than she had intended.

What if somebody breaks a rule?

I'll deal with it, Kathleen says.

Nadine raises her hand and before Kathleen acknowledges her she asks, Is it OK for us to point it out? If somebody breaks a rule?

Kathleen frowns, thinks, Get a grip. It's only week two. Since you all will be doing it, she says, I'll do the pointing out. She straightens her papers, turns to the next page in the manual. OK. First thing is to introduce yourself and tell us why you are here.

Everybody knows we're here because we have to be, Damon says. Why should anybody know anything else?

Seems a little personal, Vanessa adds.

My business is my business, Rob mutters.

Nadine scoffs, What is this, a book club?

It's in the manual, Kathleen says, holding up the booklet. It's necessary for you to take ownership of the reason you have been mandated. It doesn't have to be long, just introduce yourself and tell us why you are in this class.

For God's sake, fine. Name is Damon Sykes. I'll tell you why I'm here. It's simple. I lost my temper. One time. Really. I want you to know I was patient. I didn't fly off the handle. I take a walk, every day, in this park near my house. There are way too many stupid people with dogs. Not the dogs. The people. Stupid people who let their dogs run loose. So there's this one guy, with this big poodle. You know? Nothing but energy. So this guy walks into the park, right at the entrance, unclips the dog's leash and lets it go. Running all over the place, chasing people on bicycles, charging up to kids in strollers. Idiot owner calling Ziggy! Ziggy! Come! Ziggy never comes. So I see this go on, every day, for almost a month. Told you I was patient, right? Then this day, the damn dog comes running at me. Charging with all it's got. Standard poodle, you see it. BIG dog. I LOVE dogs. Really. Would never hurt a dog. So I stop, take the charge, the dog jumps up on my chest, knocking me into a tree. I reach around Ziggy's neck, grab his collar, wrap him into my grasp and yank down, just hard enough, not hard, really. Just hard enough to get the dog on the ground. The idiot owner comes flying up yelling, Don't you touch my dog! Don't touch my dog! When he got up to me, the dog was calmed down but the idiot kept yelling and yelling, so I let loose of the collar. Ziggy goes after a squirrel. The dog is fucking fine. The guy was still in my face, yelling, over and over, about how I hurt his dog. I just wanted to shut him up. I grabbed the leash out of his hand and, sort of, you know, wound it around his neck. Maybe choked him a little.

You can't choke somebody just a little, Rob sneers.

Only a second! Damon yells. Nothing really! He didn't black out or anything. But the idiot called the cops. Said I assaulted HIM!

But did you…Nadine presses him.

Thank you Damon, Kathleen cuts her off. Who is next?

What the hell, Nadine says. I play baseball, softball, twice a week. I was on my way to the park, crossing the street, a pretty busy street. I had the light and plenty of time. Probably about ten seconds before it was going to change. As I stepped in front of a stopped car, a silver sports car, it edged forward, just a bit. It stopped but it seemed like it could hit my leg. I jumped back, looked into the windshield. The driver looked away from me. I stared at him. Nothing. So I started to walk across the street again. After just two steps, the car edged forward again. This time I stood my ground. The car stopped. And this time I yelled, What? I could see him shrug. So I took another step, I was about two feet from the edge of the car. And he did it again! Just a little forward move, just about clipping me at the knees. I looked at him again, he looks at me, shrugs again, grins. It was the grin that got me. I stepped even with the side of the car, raised my bat and swung. Right into the passenger side headlight. No big noise, just a small splatter of plastic. He yelled something and the car moved toward me. He was steering right toward me! I stepped to the side, took a really good swing, and connected with the windshield, hit it hard enough to nearly pop my shoulder. The glass did that spider web crackling, all the way across. It was self-defense!

Way to go! Rob says. Then what?

I pounded the hood of the car, five, maybe six times. Then the cops came.

Hot damn, Vanessa says and laughs out loud.

Damon sits back in his chair, asks quietly, Why?

Nadine scowls, Why what?

Why did you keep pounding? You could have got away.

He was trying to hit me!

Did he get out of the car? Vanessa asks. Would you have hit him?

She should have! Rob says. He deserved it!

Yes! Vanessa yells. Some people deserve it. Like my shit-for-brains husband. You know what I did? I threw a suitcase at his head. Didn't really hit him. A little, but just on the ear. Wasn't much of anything. Really not much of anything. But I finally found out why he didn't want to clean that damn garage. I got fed up waiting for him to so I was out there one Saturday and he comes home, all, "hey baby, what you doing?" I had just opened his overnight bag. I wasn't looking for trouble, just seeing if there was anything in it needed to be washed. He tries to grab it off me and all this stuff, this lingerie, comes flying out. NOT mine. Not even matching! I don't wear that cheap crap. So I let go and heaved the thing at him.

Hope it was a big suitcase, Rob says.

Vanessa laughs. Sure was.

That's it? Nadine asks. Just heaved it at him?

Vanessa glares. Maybe hit him a couple of times too.

I sure as hell hope so, Nadine says.

Kathleen looks at Rob, raises her eyebrows. Well?

I am Rob Morgan. I didn't hit anybody. Or choke any-

body. I just threw something at a van because this moron of a woman wouldn't pay me for a painting. I did it
exactly like I was supposed to. She wouldn't pay me!

Damon sneers, They put you in here just for throwing something at a van?

A brick, I hit it with a brick. Broke a window.

That's all? Nadine asks.

Yeah! The painting fell on the woman. She said I hit
her with it but I didn't! It just fell against her! She should
have paid me. I did it right.

Vanessa asks sweetly, You got a story, Mrs. Morrison?

Jesus, Kathleen thinks, give me mothers and toddlers
any day. Ten minutes, she says. A ten minute break. Do
not leave the premises.

Nadine lights up and Rob joins her just outside the
front door.

A painter, huh?

Nah, that was the problem. I'm a sculptor who should
have never been painting. You, play ball?

Just for fun. Tried to get into college on a scholarship,
but none to be had. Ended up a gym teacher. You play?

Did when I was a kid.

What? Like last week?

Rob laughs. Baseball was OK but I liked football, really liked football.

No football in the girl's curriculum.

Don't I know it, Rob says as she stomps on her cigarette.

Alright, Kathleen says, listen up. She clears her throat and reads aloud:

Anger is a temporary physical and emotional state made up of feelings that vary in intensity from irritation to rage. Being in a state of anger can trigger a fight, flight or freeze response in your body. Your heart beats faster, blood flows faster, muscles get tense. In this module you will learn what anger is, how it affects your mind and body, the difference between healthy and unhealthy anger, and how to identify your triggers.

We should skip that part about learning what anger is, Rob cracks. Aren't we here because we're experts?

Screw protocol, Kathleen thinks. Well Robin, she says sweetly, if you were an expert at managing anger you wouldn't be here, would you. But maybe you can tell us where you fall on the State Trait Anger Expression Index.

Rob scowls.

Kathleen ignores her. The index measures two kinds of anger. A person with Trait Anger is one who has a constant tendency to get mad at the slightest provocation. State Anger is temporary, shows up in short outbursts, often with an understandable provocation.

That's anybody, Vanessa says. Everybody does that.

Yes, absolutely, Kathleen answers. And that's the point. Everybody gets angry. The question is how angry, how often, and how big the outburst. The goal here is to learn control of anger, not to eliminate it from your life. You all are here because of an outburst, a violent outburst.

Damon leans forward on his desk, Seems like Nadine was the most violent.

Rob yells, You're the one who choked a guy!

And there we are, Kathleen says. Thanks for the great examples. All of your stories were full of the reasons you felt you were entitled to be angry. And you most likely did have some good reasons.

Sure did, Rob mutters.

But let's look at your responses to the situations. Damon chokes, Vanessa clobbers, Nadine pounds, Rob smashes. You went from annoyed to furious in no time flat, not one of you stopped to consider the consequences of your actions. Your anger drove you to react without thinking, instead of taking time to respond appropriately.

So you're supposed to do that count to ten thing? Rob scoffs.

It's one way to slow down the reaction, Kathleen nods, but there are many other ways to cope. But first let's talk about the fact that anger is damaging you. Your mind and your body. Does anyone here have stomach problems? Ulcers?

Rob does not raise her hand.

High blood pressure? Racing heartbeats? Are you depressed? Anxious? Always irritable?

Nadine laughs, Sounds like a TV commercial for Rolaids.

Being in a constant state of anger can cause life-long health problems. Finding what triggers your anger, what causes you to fly off the handle, will help you learn to slow down your reaction time, give you time to think about your actions.

Nadine looks at her notes, says, So what if we take that time, think about it and still choke, clobber, pound or smash?

Kathleen nods. That's the thing, isn't it. Sometimes situations call for extreme measures. But most often not. It's all about what is an appropriate response.

I think smashing and clobbering is a pretty good response, Damon says.

Seems appropriate to me, Vanessa laughs.

Every time? Kathleen asks.

Of course not. Nadine says, That's ridiculous.

OK yes, Kathleen nods. So in thinking back do you think your reaction was appropriate?

Nadine shrugs, Yeah. Maybe.

Was there anything that added to, contributed to the intensity of your reaction?

Like what? Rob asks.

Like if something happened earlier that day, or something from your past reminded you of the man in the car.

Nadine shrugs. Possibly.

What else could you have done?

Why are you picking on me? Nadine barks.

Don't worry, Kathleen says, everyone will get a chance to examine their behavior. But this brings me to the reason we are here, the definition of anger management. Damon, what do you think it is?

I don't know. Learning how to not get angry.

I wish it were that easy, Kathleen says. It's not an all or nothing thing. Sometimes it's not just appropriate, but necessary to get angry.

Amen to that, Rob says.

Kathleen ignores her. Management of anger is when you are totally aware of *what* you are getting angry about, *why* you are simply annoyed, irritated, or furious, enraged. And to get to that place of understanding you have to examine your actions, get to the root of what is causing your extreme and inappropriate reactions. Because all your reactions were inappropriate and extreme. Any questions?

The group is silent.

Fine. Look at page twenty-two. For the rest of this program I want you to keep an Anger Journal. Do it like the chart in the manual. You will note when you got angry, the situation that caused it and how angry you were.

Some kind of written confession? Damon scoffs.

Think of it however you'd like. Just bring it in each week.

Rob is the last to leave the room. Mrs. Morrison, should I give you that Introduction thing from last time?

Are you finished?

Not really.

Why don't you give it to me when you're done?

There was one time we were on, if not on the team at least a team. Every year Coach set up a neighborhood flag football game during Thanksgiving break. Of course he was one of the QBs, the other selected by short straw but somehow it always ended up being Teddy Ackroyd. Us kids made a circle in the middle of the field, Coach and Teddy at either end. When a player was called they lined up behind their QB and he handed them a white or a red scrap of cloth which got stuck in the back of our pants waistband.

Teddy got first pick. He looked across at Coach, started to point at Danny. Coach coughed. Teddy spun and pointed at me. Whoops and hollers. Shouts of what do you want with that girl? More laughter. Suited me fine. The last thing I wanted was to be on Coach's team. Then, surprise surprise, Coach picked Danny. After a bunch of picks, the last one standing in the circle, Teddy's default pick, was who else but Jonah. Imagine that, Coach muttered, loud enough for all to hear. You don't have to play, you know, I told Jonah. He waved me off. It worked out that there were seven players per side, the QB and six kids ranging from fourteen to eight. I was one of the oldest and, as usual, the only girl. Coach laid down the rules. Listen up. We play for thirty minutes. Touchdown counts for seven points. Whoever is ahead at the end wins. If it's tied, it's a tie. Me and Teddy are the quarterbacks. Three of you run out for a pass, the other three are blockers or rushers. Pass rushers have to count to Mississippi five after the ball is hiked before they can charge. Only pull the flag of a player with the ball. You have to pull it all the way out. NO tackling. Ackroyd, you get the ball first. Snyder here is the referee. We go by whatever he calls. Stan Snyder, who loved his whistle, blew it loud to start the game. The parents on the sidelines cheered, sat back in their lawn chairs and passed around thermoses of Manhattans.

Teddy called us together, then checked that the flag was secure in our pants. He tugged on mine and it came loose. Here, let me set that right for you, he said quietly. I held my arms out wide while he shoved the flag deeper into my pants. Robin, Stevie and Jonah. You are the ends. Eddie, Mike and Tommy, you are the blockers. What do I do? Jonah asked. Just run out there and try to get open, doofus, Stevie says. Second play from scrimmage, Teddy lofted me a long pass. I caught it, ran it into the end zone. Coach yelled to Danny, Jesus kid! Get on her!

Coach's team scored easily on the next series. Three short passes to Danny, his brother Larry ran it in for the TD. We traded touchdown for touchdown. Nobody really playing much defense. A few running plays, mostly passes, mostly caught by Danny and me. It's tied, twenty-one all with just a minute left to play. Our team had the ball, only fifteen yards from the end zone. Coach called to Danny, pointed to me, yelled, Don't let her catch it. Danny shrugged. Coach did that throat cutting motion with his hand, the one he used to tell players to go all out. I hiked the ball, tore ass to the middle of the end zone, turned and ran smack into Danny. He knocked me down, then held his arms out, like a basketball player blocking a shot, basically sitting on me. I looked for Mr. Snyder to call interference. No call. Mississippi three...I'm sure Teddy can't even see me. At Mississippi four, Teddy must have spotted Jonah, all alone on the left, completely uncovered of course, at the one foot line. He shrugged and threw him the ball. I could tell Jonah saw it coming. He held out his hands. The ball slapped his palms hard. And then, just like I showed him, he curled it close to his chest and stepped over the goal line. Mr. Snyder finally woke up and blew the whistle. The parents on the sidelines whooped and hollered some more. What an ending! The kid came through! We all rushed over to Jonah, slapped him on the back, on the head. Jonah brushed us off, walked over to Coach, dropped the ball at his feet. You were right, he said. That is how you catch it. Coach snarled at him, then was all smiles as Teddy Ackroyd ran up. Who would have thought, Teddy said. You should have picked your own boy. Coach laughed, slapped Teddy on the back as he watched Jonah walk away.

But it didn't matter. Nothing Jonah ever did was enough, much less good enough. And I learned early on that trying to change his mind, or standing up for Jonah, only made it worse.

When Jonah was maybe eight, Coach tried to make him mow the lawn. I watched from the garage. Coach rolled the mower out onto the lawn, yelled Come here! Jonah stumbled out of the house, tripping while tying his shoes, letting the door bang shut. Coach screamed, would you pay attention! Can YOU fix that door? Jonah knew by now not to answer, that this was not a question. Coach pointed to a rubber handle. See this? Jonah nods. It's the choke. You need to push this to get it to start. And Jonah being Jonah had to ask, Why is it called a choke? What? If it helps start it, why is it called a choke? It gives it more gas. And then classic Jonah, But that's stupid. Why call it something that can kill it? How the hell do I know? Coach took Jonah's hand and shoved it onto the choke. Just push on it a few times, he said, then grab the handle of the rope and pull. Jonah pumped the choke, yanked as hard as he could on the start-er rope. It barely came half-way out, the motor sput-tered, died. Now what? he asked, More choking?

Coach pushed him aside, grabbed the rope, yanked hard once, twice, three times. on the fourth the machine roared to life and Jonah jumped back. Coach put Jonah's hands onto the handle, he was so little it barely cleared his chest. Take it, he said, just go up and back across the lawn. Jonah hunched his shoulders, gripped the handle hard, tried to hold on but the mower turned in a circle, the front end, the blade end, turning toward Coach. He shoved Jonah to the ground as he grabbed the mower's handle, guided it close to him. Jonah curled into a ball. Are you trying to kill me? Coach screamed over the sound of the mower.

And that's when I made my mistake. The only time I opened my mouth, tried to get him to change his mind. Next morning at breakfast. Coach, please, I said. You can't —Coach jerked his head up from his breakfast plate. Excuse me? It wasn't his fault, I went on. He laid down his fork and knife, said again, Excuse me. This time not a question. He's eight years old! It wasn't on purpose. I will mow—He could have taken my foot off—But—

I looked at Jonah, his head bowed, blond hair shining. He was so beautiful, looked so much like her. His teeth were clenched, willing himself not to cry. A pair of Coach's shoes were tied by the laces around his neck, sharp black heels and brown leather uppers dangled on his chest. Coach leaned back in his chair, lifted his arm high above his head, made that fist. Held it a split second, looked me right in the eye, and down it came. Plates jumped, butter knives slid sideways, knocked into glasses spilling orange juice all over the floor. Now clean this up and then go to school, he said, in a normal voice. It's for one week. If you take them off I'll know.

There was one time. Just once, that he hit me. He had an away game and wasn't supposed to be home until after ten o'clock. But something happened to the team bus and they came back just a couple of hours after they left. It wasn't like I planned some wild party. There wasn't even any party of any kind. But it was the first and only time I broke one of the cardinal rules—nobody but us allowed in the house. I asked this girl, Jill, from my art class, to come over. We weren't really friends, but at least she wasn't a cheerleader. I had told her about our great stereo or she probably wouldn't have even come. We were in the living room listening to music, laying on the rug in front of the speakers. Jonah was on the couch, drawing. I had the music cranked up really loud. Jimi Hendrix doing All Along the Watchtower. So I didn't hear when the door opened. You gotta picture it. This stupid split level house. You came in the front door and on the left was a short stairway up to the living room. I don't know how long he stood at the bottom of the stairs, watching. Jonah noticed him first, dropped his sketchpad on the rug, ran up to his bedroom. I rolled over, started to wail "There must be some kind of way outta here" and I saw him. All I could see was his head, at the top of those stairs. We looked at each other for what seemed like forever, then he walked past the stairs, into the kitchen. I jumped up, turned off the music, told Jill she had to leave, now. She got pissy, and I shoved her. Just a little. Just to try to make her move faster. She told everybody that I hit her, never talked to me again. After I got her out the door, I stood there, in the hall. For a long time. Just waiting. It was getting to be time to make dinner so I went into the kitchen. He was sitting at the table, staring at his hands. As I went to pass, to get to the fridge, he backhanded me on the side of my head. It knocked me into the counter but I didn't fall down. I put my hand on my face, turned and stared at him. And I couldn't believe it. He looked surprised, or maybe even scared. He didn't look at all like he did when he banged on the table. Or sneered at Jonah. I glared at him for a second then dropped my hand, stuck it in my pocket, turned and went upstairs. I never made dinner that night. And he ever said a word about it.

In my third year of high school I started to do what they called "act out." It was after I got out of the hospital for the ulcer thing. Not sure what changed. I had always hated anything and everything but didn't show it, kept to myself, and since I was in the same school where Coach taught I never really let myself lose it. But I started having trouble keeping it together, watched myself less, didn't even pay much attention to Jonah. I would go out, every night, after the dishes and all the other crap I had to do, and just walk, around and around those three looped streets. Once in a while I'd meet Danny and we'd play catch under the streetlights. But I finally went off in English class and this was the first time I got called to the principal's office. Mr. Bates was a new principal, much younger than the last one, which wasn't hard since the last one was about ninety. He was trying to "relate," to be cool. I didn't mean to throw the book, I told him. You threw it at Mrs. Decker's head. Not at her! It didn't hit her! I didn't mean—He gave me the side eye. We all know how well you can throw, Robin. Hoist on my own petard! I recited. You know that one? From Hamlet? Not funny, he snapped. Why did you throw the book at her? It was just a paperback, Of Mice and Men. It's not even very long. He tilted his head. I got fed up with her, I said. She kept going on and on about how complicated the relationship was between Lennie and George. Was it moral for George to kill Lennie. And, he asked? It's NOT complicated! George HAS to kill Lennie. It's the only way he can protect him. I just wanted her to shut up. Why are you yelling? I'm not! Did it work? Throwing the book? I smiled. Kind of. I'm here listening to you instead of her. Again. Not funny. You've got some temper on you. He held up a file folder. You have a file on me? There have been other reports. What reports? He thumbed through the file. Elbowing a girl out of line...She cut in front! Tripping Melissa...She cheated, tried to copy my test! Shoving a boy at the drinking fountain...He was making fun of Jonah! Growling at..NAH, growling? Come on! He closed the file, tossed it on his desk. You're a good little athlete. Why aren't you on a team? What, field hockey? What's wrong with field hockey? Field hockey is just an opportunity to beat the crap out of somebody's shins with a big stick. What good is a game where you can't throw the ball. Have you talked with Miss Harmonas about college? With your grades you'll be able to snag a great scholarship. Probably a full ride. I'm not sure, I said. Maybe I shouldn't go. Jonah is— Jonah is not a kid. He has Coach. But he's—He's not your responsibility. You don't understand. You have to live your life, Robin. Before I could stop myself I said, But it's not safe. He leaned toward me, said quietly. Not safe. How? I opened my mouth, felt Coach close behind me, his arms on my shoulders, fingers digging into my neck, his voice in my ear whispering Our business is our business. Nobody tells anybody our business. Nothing, I said, it's nothing. I struck a pose, I'm just being dramatic. You're sure? Sure I'm sure. The intercom buzzed. School Board meeting in twenty minutes, Mr. Bates. He took my file, stuck it in a cabinet behind him. Alright, Robin. You have to apologize to Mrs. Decker, in front of the class, and I'm giving you a week's detention. He stood up and put on his suit jacket. You're lucky I don't suspend you. It's only because you're Coach's daughter. Why don't you join a team, he said, or try out for cheerleading. Do something to burn off all that energy. What are you so mad at anyway?

G race clears their dishes from the dining table, says over her shoulder as she passes through the swinging door into her kitchen, You sure you can't go? I told everybody about us. I want my friends to meet you. I promise this production will be a lot better than the Titus.

Rob makes a split second decision not to tell her about Anger Management. Can't. I have a meeting that night, just for a few more weeks.

A meeting? What you up to? Grace pours the last of the wine into Rob's glass. I'm guessing it's not AA.

Nah, nothing like that. She scans Grace's apartment quickly, spies the Ansel Adams photo over the fireplace. I'm taking a class, she lies, in photography.

Where?

Down by me. Cooper Union.

I thought you hated school.

It's just one class.

I'd be happy to help, you know. If you want more classes. Maybe uptown, at Barnard? That's where I went. You could stay here—

Rob pushes away from the table. I'm good where I am. I promised Donald and Maria I'd take care of their place.

Maybe when they get back?

Yeah, sure, she says. We can talk about it more later. Lemme help you wash the dishes.

Grace takes Rob's arms, drapes them around her neck. I'd rather you wash my back. Time for a bath?

Rob slides her arms down to Grace's hips, lifts her into the air, says, Always time for a bath. You got all the hot water in the world.

I love it, Grace says as she throws her legs around Rob's waist, how strong you are. She buries her face in Rob's neck. You actually sweep me off my feet!

You are amazing, Grace takes the towel off her wet hair. Sure you can't stay over?

Gotta go, says, Rob grabs her jacket, I'm working on some new ideas. She kisses Grace on the forehead.

Let me give you cab fare. It's Sunday. All those rowdy football fans will be on the train. Can you believe believe how many people love that barbaric crap?

Yeah, who could believe that, Rob answers, I'm fine on the subway, just fine. Let me know how the play was. As she rides the elevator down she thinks, rowdy and barbaric, not so sure about the rowdy part, but you could definitely call me barbaric.

Only one more after this, Damon says.

Thank God, Vanessa sighs, I'm tired of driving to this lousy neighborhood.

This? Rob scoffs, a neighborhood? There's no neighborhood here, it's a lousy suburb.

Still in the city, Damon says.

Where are you living, Staten Island?

Bronx, for your information. Near the Zoo.

Fits, Rob says under her breath.

Damon leans over his desk, turns to Rob, yells, What'd I ever do to you?

Tsk. Tsk. Nadine says, Sounds like someone is pushing a nine.

Kathleen comes in. I assume you are all doing your Anger Journal? We'll work from that today. And I'll give more information later, but our last class will not be here, but in lower Manhattan.

Hallelujah! Rob says.

What the hell are we going to do down there?

Later, Damon, Kathleen says. Now, everybody up. Move the desks to the sides of the room.

Scraping, screeching, they move the desks to clear the center. They stand awkwardly, fidgeting, not looking at each other.

Now what? Nadine asks.

This is what, Kathleen says. I want each of you to read me one entry from your Anger Journal. And tell me how you rated it on the scale.

Anything?

Anything at all.

Rob says, I got mad when I was buying subway tokens and this guy cut in front of me in line. It was a 3, more like between a 3 and 4.

Kathleen writes it on the board.

A man who held up the bus, wouldn't get on, one foot on the steps, one on the street, holding up the whole bus for his friend, Nadine says. I put it at a 4.

Next, Kathleen says as she lists it on the blackboard.

Damon flips through a few pages of his log. A woman walking her dog, just left it on the sidewalk, didn't even push it to the curb. Curb your dog signs all over the place! But no, just left it on the sidewalk. Rated it 5.

What's with you and dogs? Rob mutters.

Over her shoulder as she writes, Kathleen says, Vanessa?

I haven't been mad much lately, now that that idiot is out of my life. But I wrote about when everybody asks me how I'm doing? Makes me crazy. How the hell do they think I'm doing?

Your ratings? Kathleen asks.

Usually a 2 or 3, once in a while a 5.

Excellent, let's start with that one. What do you think made the difference in your rating?

I don't know...depended on who was doing the asking.

I can see that, Nadine says. Be different depending on the motive of the asker.

Exactly! Vanessa says, some of them don't want to do anything but rub my nose in it.

So let's act one out, Kathleen says.

Act it out? Damon groans, You kidding?

Not kidding, Kathleen walks over and points, Rob, you play Vanessa. Vanessa, you play someone you rated a 5. Come on, come into the middle of the room.

Rob takes a few steps forward, puts her hands on her hips, hunches her shoulders.

I don't do that! Vanessa says.

Sure do, Nadine laughs.

Damon and Kathleen nod in agreement.

Vanessa walks up to Rob, says in a mincing voice. So sorry, Vanessa. I heard about you and Calvin. But I told you all along, you are better off without him.

Rob gets right in her face, yells. You never said anything such thing. But you are damn right! I sure as hell am better off!

Nervous laughter.

Kathleen asks, Vanessa, is that a five response? Is that what you might have done?

It's right on, Vanessa laughs.

So why is that a five? Five is pretty serious. Why was there an anger response at all?

She was...she didn't have to bring it up.

Maybe she was being nice? Nadine asks.

Nah, she just wanted to make me feel bad.

Maybe you're just still mad at Calvin, Damon says.

Vanessa stalks up to him, God damn right I am!

He holds up his hands, Well don't take it out on me.

Bingo, Kathleen says quietly. One of the biggest and most important things you can take away from this program, an understanding of displacement.

They all just stare at her.

It's redirecting your anger at something, something that is not so threatening, or painful. Usually someone who doesn't even deserve it. It's a defense mechanism, a way of not processing your real emotion. And it mostly comes out in the form of aggression.

Can we sit down now? Damon asks quietly.

Not yet. Let's move on. We'll do Nadine next. Vanessa, you are Nadine, Damon, you be the guy who held up the bus.

After the group works through all the scenarios, Kathleen points to the board. So. Rob. Why were you angry at the guy who cut in front of you?

He was a jerk! It wasn't fair!

True, Kathleen says. Any other possible reasons?

Nadine says, Maybe he was sick?

Vanessa says, Maybe his kid was sick?

Kathleen says, Or maybe he was just a jerk.

Right! Rob says.

But why does what he did have to affect you at all?

Because it wasn't fair!

What did you feel at the time?

Angry! What the hell else?

No, I mean in your body, what did you feel? Were you short of breath? Jaw clenched? Muscles tensed? Did you want to hurt him? Did you think about him for a while afterward?

Rob sits back in her chair. All right, all right, I get it. Maybe it wasn't worth it. That time.

It was so not worth it, Kathleen says. If you always get that mad at little things like this you'll give yourself a heart attack. Or get ulcers.

Rob snaps her head up. I'm fine, she says. But I get it. I get it.

And Nadine—

I get it too. You don't have to spell it out. Mine was a classic example of displacement. I hated the guy, the guy in the suit, holding up the bus. He was all the men who get promoted before me, whose stupid ideas I have to listen to every day. That guy in the car, edging me out.

You're a quick learner, Vanessa says.

Nadine waves her off. Nah, just connecting the dots.

And you Mr. Dog poop? Rob says.

Damon scowls. It's not about the fucking dog! It's about doing the right thing. Playing by the rules. I DO have ulcers. I hate everybody!

The room is silent. Kathleen walks slowly, stands by Damon.

I'm not gonna hit—

She puts her hand on his shoulder, says, I know, Damon, I know you aren't.

So what are we supposed to do? he asks quietly.

To start, Kathleen answers, you learn to cope, to change your responses, slow down your reactions so you can remember what you are really angry about.

And then? Rob asks.

Then you try to find the root of your anger.

Can we take a break?

No, Kathleen says as she passes out a half-sheet of paper, We're actually almost out of time. This is where we will be meeting next week, for our last session.

A Meditation Studio? Damon says. Are you kidding?

You asked for some solutions, Kathleen says, erasing the blackboard. Meditation is a proven stress reliever, sure to be useful in coping with your anger.

And it's in my neck of the woods, Rob mutters to herself. Farewell Queens. Parting is no fucking sorrow whatsoever.

Mick and Rob walk down Canal Street, into China-town. He asks, Why do you keep making notes on that thing?

I'm supposed to keep track of when I get mad. And how mad I get. It's the last of my homework. I am being good and handing in my homework.

You're mad? Now? About what?

She laughs to herself, thinking of Damon, says, That guy with the dog, up in front of us. He's walking so slow, taking up the whole sidewalk.

Are you in a hurry?

No, but.

So how mad are you?

On a scale of 1 to 10, about a 3.

Robbie, you wake up at 5.

Hah! Yeah, but see, it's working. I used to rate it as a 4. And when I'm writing it down, I'm not yelling at the asshole.

So you are getting something out of that class?

I never needed to be in it in the first place, I only went to get out of jail.

Have you told your Grace about it?

She's not my—

Have you?

Yeah. Sort of. Not really.

Well?

Well it's embarrassing!

She's a shrink, she'll—

Exactly! I don't want to get shrunk.

Did they have you write anything else?

Nothing important. I wrote stuff about my life, my life before I met you.

You had a life? Before me?

She punches him in the shoulder. So who is the next show?

Thomas. A good painter.

Thomas who?

Just goes by one name.

Like Charo?

Turn onto Pell Street, I like that place downstairs. So can I read it?

No. Maybe. I'll see. It's not done.

Kathleen waits in her car thinking Damn, the city really cheaped out using this vendor. She jumps, nearly spilling coffee down her blouse when Vanessa taps on her window.

This is the place? Vanessa asks, Seriously?

Getting out of her car, Kathleen nods, Looks like it.

Damon pulls up across the street, waits until Kathleen motions him to come over. Rob turns the corner and joins them.

My car is alright here? Damon asks.

Vanessa huffs, Your Nissan will be fine.

Rob chuckles, What could happen?

Nadine walks up. What kind of New Yorkers are you? You people don't know what a subway is?

What's the address, Rob asks Kathleen.

Over there, near the corner of Wooster Street.

You live around here? Vanessa asks.

Rob nods, Greene and Prince. THIS is a neighborhood.

A hand-lettered yellow and red sign, MEDITATION, is taped to the black steel door. Kathleen presses the buzzer on a rusty panel beside it. They hear a bell, like an old fashioned fire alarm bell, ring loudly. After a few, long, minutes the door opens and there stands a tall blue-eyed man, dressed in baggy dark blue pants and an orange long-sleeved cotton shirt that ties on the side. It's hard to guess his age, somewhere in his forties, maybe fifties, his thick wiry blond hair at odds with the craggy, lined face. His necklace of wooden beads falls forward as he bows and says, Welcome. I am Jasper. Please come in. His voice is rich, deep, soothing.

But nobody moves.

Kathleen says, Is this the right place? We are with City Services.

He nods, Yes, yes. Please, come in.

Well come on, Rob says, smiling at Jasper as he leads them into a musty hallway, buckling red linoleum, cracked dingy plaster walls. Up a short flight of stairs on the left is an elevator cage.

I'm not getting in that, Vanessa says.

It's the top floor, Jasper says. I could walk with you. It's only three flights but the steps are steep.

Not walking, Kathleen says. Let's do this.

Jasper pulls back the collapsible door. They step onto the elevator, the floor shifts like a small moored boat.

Closing the door, Jasper says, It's sturdy but kind of slow.

Vanessa moans.

The elevator rises past visibly huge timbers, cracked plaster, electrical conduits. The lift makes a scraping screech and Vanessa moans again. They come to rest with a jolt, the metal clatters as Jasper pulls back the gate. The step off into a small hallway.

Jasper opens another black metal door. Please, he says again, smiling a huge welcoming smile, It's all right. Come in.

They shuffle out of the dank, gloomy space and are stopped in their tracks.

Oh wow, Rob says.

Oh wow indeed, Nadine whispers.

Thank God, Kathleen says under her breath.

It was as if they had stepped into a canyon of light. Along the entire back wall of the empty space are huge windows, each at least ten feet tall, three feet wide. The sun creates slanted, geometric grids of wavering light on the polished wooden floor. In front of the windows is a wall of green in terracotta pots— jade plants, spider plants, sprawling ferns, long, leggy philodendra, rubber trees.

This room must be a hundred feet long, Damon says.

And it smells so good, Vanessa says.

Jasper smiles. The plants purify the air, he says quietly. And I burn incense, of course. He slips out of his flip-flops saying, If you would take off your shoes and follow me?

Rob and Nadine slip off their boots.

Just do it, Kathleen says to the others.

After a lot of shuffling and grumbling, they leave their shoes at the door then follow Jasper to the center of the room. Five flat cushions covered with the same blue cloth as Jasper's pants are laid in a straight line on the floor. He nods to the group, inviting them with a wave to take a seat with their backs to the windows. Rob, Vanessa and Nadine chose a cushion. Vanessa lowers herself awkwardly and sticks her legs straight out, sets her large purse on her lap and closes her arms around it.

Nadine and Rob kneel easily, shift to a cross-legged position. Damon looks around, No chair? Jasper smiles and shakes his head. Damon scowls, lowers himself and sits, knees up, leaning back on his hands.

Kathleen says, No no, I am not in the group. I will watch from over there.

Jasper smiles and shakes his head again. All must sit, he says, sweetly. There are no observers here.

Kathleen crosses her arms over her chest, hands clench her file folders. Maybe I could see some documentation, Mr. Jasper. Do you have the...

Jasper smiles hugely. Of course, come with me. And please, it's just Jasper.

They walk to a beaded curtain doorway to the left of the front door. A mattress on the floor covered with a patchwork quilt takes up most of the room, a small metal desk is in the corner. Over it hangs several framed documents, all in a language Kathleen cannot read.

Is this your first time working with City Services?

No, no, Jasper says. I've done several youth groups.

But never with adults in an Anger Management Program?

Not as yet. But it can't be different. Meditation is meditation.

She points to the wall, These say you are qualified?

Oh yes! I've been meditating and teaching for over twenty years. In the States, in India.

You are by yourself here?

He nods.

Kind of a dicey area to start a business, isn't it?

He smiles that lovely smile again. It was in my price range.

Kathleen pulls a paper from the folder thinks, I should check this out at the office but remembers that she doesn't really care anymore and says, Fine. Just sign this form for me and let's get started.

He nods as he signs the form. This will get my fee released?

Yes, as soon as I process it.

I am grateful, he says and parts the beaded curtain, ushering her out.

What, Rob says. He's so calm. What's not to like?

Vanessa scoffs, Something's off.

Damon nods. Way too smiley.

Hey, it's better than role playing each other's Anger Journal, Nadine says.

Can't argue with that, Vanessa says.

As Kathleen and Jasper come back, Damon pats the cushion beside him.

It's a matter of trust, he says and grins at Kathleen.

She scowls, lowers herself onto the pillow saying, Somebody is going to have to help me up.

Jasper goes to a low table under the center window, takes up a small tray and a cushion. He sets the cushion on the floor facing the group, sinks down as if he had no bones. His back is ramrod straight, but not stiff, his hands rest easily on his thighs. He raises his hands as if in prayer and bows.

Again, welcome, he says. I feel very fortunate that you are here. I have practiced meditation for over twenty years, in the States and overseas. I use modalities from all over the world. The technique we will be practicing is based on the breath, a kind of circular breathing. You breathe slowly and deeply through your nose, pull the air way down, feel your belly filling up. Then let it out, collapse your belly, feel the air come up your lungs and out your nose. Make your in-breath the same length as your out-breath, with no break in between. No holding your breath. Try to think only about your breath, feel it coming in and going out, follow it in your mind. If you think other things, it's OK, don't worry, just come back to thinking about your breath.

That's all? Vanessa asks.

Damon seconds. We're just going to breathe?

Jasper smiles. Yes, that's all, he says.

How is that going to help? Damon asks

Well, let's find out. Make sure you are comfortable. If you need to stretch out your legs, that's fine.

Vanessa lays her purse behind her, Kathleen sets the file folder on her lap. The others shift, sit still.

OK? Jasper asks, then nods his head at each person individually. They nod back. Now we will be quiet. Close your eyes. Breathe in.

They all take a breath.

Now everybody breathe out.

They exhale. Kathleen and Damon cough, Vanessa blows out like she is swimming laps.

Jasper whispers, Slower. In breath same as out breath.

Each person struggles to take a longer, deeper breath.

Again, Jasper says quietly. Even slower.

Their breathing sounds less ragged, quieter.

Better. Keep going.

They breathe, in and out, over and over, until finally they breathe in unison. Even Damon crosses his legs, his hands on his thighs, mimicking Jasper's pose.

Good, Jasper says. It's sounding good. It's starting to work. Keep your eyes closed, keep breathing, in and out. In and out.

The sunlight warms their backs, the silence broken only by the sound of breath in their ears. A stillness, something deeper than simply the stillness of silence and sunlight, fills the room. Over and over, breathing together. Then a ping, one single tone that takes them all away from their breath.

It's good, all good, Jasper says. Go back to your breath. Keep breathing. All is well.

Once again, they resume the rhythmic inhaling, exhaling. Another ping. This one deeper, richer, followed by several more, slowly and evenly spaced. The tones fluctuate, echo each other, then resolve into a swirling humming sound, unifying the notes. It is like being on a roller coaster made of sound, short ups, big downs, swinging wide over empty space, sliding up only to fall again.

Whoa, whoa, Damon says. What the hell is that!

Everybody opens their eyes.

I'm dizzy, Vanessa and Nadine say in unison.

Rob nods, Weird.

Very, Kathleen said.

Jasper is smiling. He holds up a wooden mallet partially covered with a band of leather and a metal bowl. He strikes the bowl, a single tone, then strokes the edge of the bowl with the mallet, around and around, creating the wavering, wobbling sound.

What the hell is that? Vanessa echoes Damon.

A Singing Bowl, Jasper answers. It is a terrific tool.

What for, Kathleen asks.

Going deep into yourself. Using vibration. It's about the power of vibration, how sound can have deeply meaningful effects on your mind and body. Jasper hands the bowl to Kathleen. You all felt it, yes? You see it's just a metal bowl but when used properly it can be very powerful. When we combine visualization with the sounds of the bowl, when you allow the vibrations into your body, it can resonate with your soul, take you to a place of deep understanding.

Damon shakes his head saying, I didn't sign up for any religious stuff.

It's not religious, by soul I mean your innermost being. It's not just an eastern idea. A Swiss doctor, Hans Jenny, did a lot of research into cymatics. The tones set up what's called a frequency following response. It creates a balance between the two halves of your brain. The sounds tune you in to the universal sound that is inside you and outside you. It's been scientifically proven that sound can be transformative, that sound can heal.

Kathleen hands back the bowl, This is a module in an Anger Management Course. We are supposed to—

Jasper nods. Yes! There is too much anger in the world. Meditation can help so much. We don't have to use the bowl, we can simply breathe. That is also a very helpful tool. But this, he holds up the bowl and mallet, this is like a jet plane. Gets you there faster. It's up to you all. Do you want to do more?

They all look at Kathleen. She shrugs, We have to stay the whole time to fulfill the requirement. How long was what we just did?

A little under twenty minutes.

That's all?

He smiles. It always seems longer. You are all doing so well. Let's do a bit more. This time, please, move your cushions, make a circle.

We have to get up?

And down again?

Just do what he says, Kathleen says. Damon, give me a hand.

Closer, a little closer, Jasper says. Make it a tighter circle. He lights a stick of incense, sets it in the center of the circle. The smoke floats upward, then disperses over their heads. That's good, he says. Perfect. So are we good using the bowl?

Kathleen looks around the circle. They all shrug. Sure, why not, she says.

They sit so closely their knees almost touch. Rob gives Nadine the side-eye. She smirks.

OK, Jasper says, Here we go.

Everybody shifts on their cushions, closes their eyes.

Breathing in.

Breathing out.

Follow your breath, Jasper says in a near whisper, but also look inside. Remember. See yourself as a child. Have compassion for that child.

Breathing in.

Breathing out.

Many minutes of breathing in, breathing out.

Then come the tones and they know it is just a wooden mallet being rubbed on the edge of a metal bowl. The sounds float in the air, weave into the smoke. There is a hitch, a gasp, as they all fall farther into the tones. Their breathing becomes ragged, but evens out as the sounds continue to enfold them. Rob senses a sliding apart inside her, then a re-forming, as if she, like the tones, is being woven. She panics, her breathing goes out of synch, but the tones pull her back. A wave of fear, of nausea, passes through her, but she cannot resist. She follows the tones and hears, senses, does not understand.

a little girl is standing outside the bathroom, pounding on the locked door. let me in! you have to let me in! not now sweetie, I'm OK. but the water, Mommy, the water is coming from under the door. baby, I'm fine, don't worry. We're just fine.

That never happened! Rob jerks awake, becomes aware that she has just yelled.

Jasper wraps his hands around the bowl, killing the sound. Are you alright?

Damon rolls sideways, mutters, Why'd you mess that up? I was liking it.

Nadine rubs her eyes, lets out a huge breath. Those tones. Amazing. I can see how this could help.

Vanessa sighs deeply, cradles her bag close to her chest.

What is it? Jasper whispers to Rob, what happened.

Rob is bent over, clutching her stomach. Her mouth is dry, ears pulsing with the tones of the bowl, the sound of running water.

Ok, we're done here, Kathleen says.

There is still time, Jasper says.

No, we're done.

Are you sure—

Kathleen rolls on to her hands and knees, yells, Enough! Time to go!

Rob's hands are still shaking but she works to bring the world back in balance, says with a smirk, Is that an appropriate reaction, Mrs. Morrison?

Just get me up and let's get out of here.

Rob looks at Damon, at Vanessa and Kathleen, watches them struggle to get off the floor. She tries to get Nadine's attention. What the fuck, she thinks, nobody else saw anything?

Jasper lays his hand on Rob's shoulder, Are you alright?

She ducks away, shakes her head.

Please, stay, Jasper says to her, cradling the bowl to his chest.

Not now.

At the door, hopping, leaning on the brick wall, they struggle into their shoes, laughing, glad the whole thing is over.

Jasper forces a smile, says to Kathleen, Thank you again for coming...you will send in the papers?

Don't worry. Nothing will get in the way of this being my last official act.

Jasper takes the elevator down, slowly, very slowly, to the ground floor. They hit bottom with a bump. Vanessa moans. The black steel door sticks. Kathleen gives it a good yank and they are back in the world, on the grimy sidewalk, avoiding piles of dog shit, avoiding eye contact. She hands out sealed envelopes containing their certificates of completion. They accept the envelopes, making sure each gets the right one.

Rob holds out her sketchbook. Mrs. Morrison, do you want this? That Introduce Yourself thing?

Kathleen sneers, Good little girl, need to hand in your homework?

Jesus! She shoves the book in her bag, Where did nice Mrs. Morrison go?

Kathleen smiles. Anger management, Rob, try counting to ten. Alright, all done here people, she says as she gets in her car. Damon and Vanessa follow and they all drive off.

Rob looks back at the building, yearning for the voice of a ghost. When she sees Nadine head uptown on West Broadway, she turns back to the building. Straining to hear, *don't worry baby, I'm fine,* she punches the bell. The door opens immediately.

I knew you'd be back, Jasper says.

Knew how? Rob says suspiciously.

Come upstairs.

They ride the elevator in silence, sit on the cushions and Jasper hands her a cup of water.

So? he asks.

You don't know?

It's for you to tell me.

Shit. I don't know how to say it. When you were doing that thing with the bowl. I went somewhere, heard things, saw things, felt things.

He nods. Yes?

I heard my mother. Heard her say something, something she never said.

More likely you remembered something you'd forgotten. The vibrations set up by the bowl can take us deep inside ourselves. I did prompt you to remember yourself as a child.

Why? Why that thing about being a child?

A lot of angry adults grow up in homes filled with anger, angry people.

So?

It can carry over. What did you hear?

She lays her hands on her eyes, then over her ears, shakes her head, says I KNOW that never happened. I never heard that. Never was in that place.

I see you really believe that—

I'm telling you! I was never there!

OK. I believe you.

You don't, but I don't give a fuck.

I see why you are in anger management. Do you have dreams often? Dreams you remember?

Nah, I sleep pretty hard. I mostly remember stuff when I'm awake, go into these daydream-like spaces. But this was different. I felt this thing, like it was happening to all of us but when it was over it nobody seemed shook. It looked like I was the only one it happened to. How come?

The bowl works differently on everyone. Most people simply enjoy the sounds, for others the tones take them deeper. Some let themselves be open but close it off quickly. You must be very open, open to hearing what's in your head. Do you consider yourself to be introspective? Maybe empathetic?

Ha! Don't think anyone would use either of those words for me.

Maybe not on the surface—

I want more. With the bowl. Can we do it again? Can we do it now?

I have sessions on Wednesdays at 6:30, when I use the bowl.

Nah, nah. I'm not good in groups. She points to the bowl and mallet resting on the cushion beside her. Where can I get one of those?

You can buy a bowl anywhere, but you won't be able to do much with it.

Yeah?

You want more of what you experienced? Come to my class. We can see if you have what it takes.

To?

Set up the right vibrations, to learn to make the connections.

Mick snatches a French fry from Rob's plate. So you're free and clear, yes?

She slides the plate closer to her side of the table.

It's been ages. I miss you, kiddo.

Been busy.

I sold two more pieces from *Catch*. He hands her a wad of cash. Here's your cut.

She shoves the money in her pocket without counting it. Thanks, Mick, she smiles. So I'm rich?

You look tired. You OK? What you been up to?

Working, she lies, working a lot.

On? He grabs her pickle spear, takes a bite, lays it back on her plate.

For fuck's sake!

She looks across at him as he sucks pickle juice off his fingers, dressed to the nines in the middle of the day in the middle of the week. Beautiful. Even when he doesn't try. She wants him, even when she doesn't want him.

Your place? she says.

He smiles, says to the back of a passing waiter, Check please, then to Rob, You're rich now, you get this.

As she pays the cashier she whispers to Mick's back, Why should we rise because 'tis light? Did we lie down because t'was night?

Jasper gently pulls her fingers away from the bowl. Keep your palm open, let the bowl rest easily, but support it. You are strong, you can keep your arm stable.

It's the first time in two months that he has let her hold a bowl. Rob's hand is shaking, from excitement as much as the difficulty of holding her hand steady. I'm just—

I know, he says, I know. Here, hold the mallet in the center. No, don't move it yet, just feel it, just hold it.

Alright, alright. She breathes as he has taught her, tries to calm her mind.

Now, one tap. Tap softly.

The bowl barely rings.

A little harder.

The second ping is clear, steady.

Now, clockwise around the rim, keep the mallet vertical. Use your whole arm, like stirring a pot of soup.

The tones are faint.

More pressure, he says, just enough to make the sound, not enough to dislodge the bowl. Slowly, no hurry. That's better.

She knows she is sitting still, that her arm is in motion, but the tones pull her away from herself for just a second and her breath loses its rhythm, the mallet falls from her hand.

Shit!

He takes the bowl and mallet, sets them on the cushion beside him. Told you it wasn't easy. You'll get better. You've got a nice touch. These last few weeks in class, did you have an experience like the first time? See anything, hear anything?

Nah. Nah, nothing new, she lies.

Because she can't find words to explain it, can't understand it and doesn't like to think about it, she has never told him how she mostly checks out during the classes. The flood of sensations she felt during the first group session has caused her to go back to her tried and true method of counting in her head to block things out. She doesn't want to lose herself sitting in a group of strangers. Although she has been physically present, she had been essentially absent.

No, she repeats, Not getting anything I already didn't already remember.

What do you think this is? A seance? Your mother talking to you from the "other side?" It's you, what's in you, talking to yourself. It's all in your head.

Like hell! I'm not making it up.

I'm sorry, he laughs, a little meditation humor. Couldn't resist.

Ha fucking ha.

But I mean it, Rob, what you are seeing, hearing, is already in your head.

Then my head is wrong.

He laughs, You said it, I didn't.

Dust has settled on Rob's work bench. It's been several weeks since she has picked up any tools. She wanders around the loft poking in drawers that she had never touched, opening closets, and finds a case of Plastilina Modeling Clay. A soft grey-green, the clay is stiff but eases up as she holds it, warms it. She used this once, in an art class, liked the feel of it on her hands. After a couple of drinks she pulls out the worn duffel bag, opens the portfolio. She takes out Jonah's notebook, thumbs through the violent drawings of Coach. The whiskey bottle is empty of all but that tiny bit, down at the corner. Rob upends it, nearly missing her mouth. Jonah would be fifteen today. Her guts churn when she can't block out their last conversation. She unwraps a block of clay, rips off a jagged hunk.

he keeps playing it. over and over, the same damn thing. we gotta get out of this place, if it's the LAST thing—Jonah! For Christs sake! how many time are you going to play that! it's a tape loop, he comes down from upstairs, holding a tape recorder. don't you like The Animals? where did you get that? Mr. Jaworski. the art teacher? he nods, presses play, turns up the volume. we gotta get out of this place, if it's the LAST thing—we gotta get out of this place, if it's the LAST thing— turn it down! he shrugs, lowers the volume. for Christs sake why don't you just play the whole damn thing? then it wouldn't be a loop, would it. it's about editing, choosing, taking the parts that mean the most. it's annoying—no! it's powerful. a statement! did you do your math homework? fuck that. I'm gonna be an artist. you don't need to go to school to be an artist. you're not gonna be anything unless you get out of high school. what about you? you know, I'm doing the stupid college thing. I know you haven't he says slyly. haven't what? applied anywhere. you look at my mail? I look at everything. so? what are you gonna do after graduation? not sure. Jonah takes the tape out of the recorder, slides it back and forth across the table. you really like him? what? who? come on, Danny, who else? he's the only one you told, about how she called you Puck, where we lived. he's been my friend since forever. of course I like him. but do you like him like him. Jesus Christ, don't be a moron, you sound as stupid as Teen magazine. he stops sliding the tape across the table, says, and you sound just like Coach. she turns, points at him with the knife she is using to cut an onion for the meatloaf, hisses, don't you ever say that again. he falls back, slumps in his chair, his mouth set hard, but his eyes tear up. Jonah, I'm sorry. please, don't cry. fuck off, he says. it's from the onion.

She sees that her hands have formed a bird with the clay, not unlike the ones she carved in Tompkins Square Park. Sitting cross-legged on the bed, she sets the bird bowl on her palm, strokes it with a pretend mallet, straining to hear the sounds.

It's late spring, the afternoon sun is strong, the air still cool in the shadows. Rob sees Seymour sitting on an upturned bucket outside the door to their building.

Thank god you're here! she yells. I was over by the river. This thing has been following me. I can't get it to go away.

He sets a screwdriver and rag onto his lap, peers at the dog, Might need some work.

Rob points to the ribs showing even through the long tangled black hair. Is it sick? I don't know why it's been following me, for at least twenty blocks.

Looks hungry. What are you going to do?

I don't want a dog! I don't know anything about—

This dog needs help.

Who doesn't?

He's a beaut, could be a Belgian.

What should I do?

Give him a little food, then a bath, feed him some more, see how it goes.

Yeah, but how do I get rid of him if it doesn't "go" well?

I'm thinking it will go fine. What's his name?

How the hell do I know?

So give him one. What would you call him?

Rob steps back, takes a long look at the dog. Its tail is tucked, ears flopped to the sides of its head, but its eyes look right at her. She doesn't know if it is pleading with her, or daring her.

Benny, I'd call him Benny.

As in Goodman? Benny The Torch?

Who? No, as in Benvolio, from Shakespeare.

He stole that.

The dog?

Shakespeare. From a Matteo Bandello story.

The Benvolio I know was the guy who tried to make peace, between the Montagues and Capulets.

Same guy, he says. Benvolio. Better than Malvolio.

She smiles, Way better than that slimeball.

He stole that story too. From Barnabe Rich via Bandello.

You lost me, she says as she opens the building door. What the hell, at least I can feed it.

Benny is wolfing down the remains of a hamburger when Seymour carries a crumpled shoe box into Rob's loft, sets it on the kitchen table. Put a little warm water in the tub, he says. Help him jump in. Yeah, yeah, he croons. See? What a beautiful dog.

Maybe you should take him?

He followed you, you got picked.

She pours water over Benny's back with a jelly glass, rubs a small dollop of shampoo into his fur. The dog is patient, still, closes his eyes.

He loves you already. This is a great dog. Obviously well trained. Definitely Belgian, look at those ears, probably a Groenendael.

How do you know that?

I said, from Belgium.

No, how do you know—

I said! from Belgium.

You were there?

How many times do I have to say it?

Seymour, where the hell haven't you been?

Nepal. I got a leash and collar, a brush, you'll need to brush him a lot. And clippers.

For?

Toe nails. You like walking?

Yeah. You know I'm always walking.

You'll need to walk more.

You had a dog?

What you don't know, he whispers.

What? What don't I know?

He's smart, really smart. And sensitive. You be nice around him, gentle.

I'm not so good at nice.

I know.

As he enters the loft, Benny sniffs Mick's shoes once, bumps into his knee, turns and walks back toward Rob.

I still can't get used to it, Mick says.

"It" is Benny. Get used to it.

Rob and Benny have figured it out. Soon after the dog's arrival, just a couple of months ago, Seymour dropped off a fifty pound bag of dog food and a book with its back cover missing, *Care and Feeding of German Shepherds*. The note stuck in the book read, "It was the closest country I could find." After the first few dicey days, Benny pooping in the loft, cringing in the corner, Rob has learned his signals, pays great attention to his needs. Once she stopped worrying that she was doing everything wrong it didn't take long for them to connect. He trusts her completely now, she reaches for him on the big bed, listens for his soft snoring. They wake early, go for a walk. Seymour gave her a chewed-up rubber ball, Benny taught her to play fetch in Sara Roosevelt Park. She is thrilled to throw something, didn't realize how much she missed throwing a ball, any ball. She brushes him every day, his coat is full and shiny, black as coal. His ears stand at attention. When she is working in the studio he lays on a bundle of blankets she bought at the army surplus store. And he watches her, closely. His eyes are almond shaped, deep brown. A small patch on his muzzle is the only white fur on his seventy pound body. When she gets angry, loses her temper, yells, he lays back his ears, cowers behind the bathtub until she notices he is gone. She coaxes him out, feeling like shit, apologizing. Not wanting to scare him, she watches herself. She is eating better, more regularly. Drinking less. On the last walk before bed they head north, check out the pickup basketball game at The Cage on West 4th, stroll past Rob's old house. They sit on the curb sometimes, Benny leaning into her side listening attentively to her recite Puck's lines. Lord, what fools these mortals be! She reaches around his broad chest, pulls him close, whispers, And yet, to say the truth, reason and love keep little company nowadays.

Mick holds up two wine glasses. You going uptown on me?

Grace brought them. Says it tastes better.

Holding up an empty bottle, he murmurs, And expensive wine.

Rob takes the bottle, sets it under the counter. I like it. She likes it.

She must really like it. What are there, twelve empties here?

I mostly visited her before. But with Benny she's over here lately. A lot.

You in love?

Again? You're the one who told me to be nice to her!

How nice can you be, kiddo?

Who's your latest? What's her name?

So Robbie's in love?

What the fuck Mick. Why do you even care?

He sits down on her bed, unties his shoes, sighs, Sorry. Really, I'm sorry. It's Thomas.

The soon-to-be-famous one-named painter?

The second show was a bust.

Did he throw something at Stevenson too?

Mick laughs, I wish. The work stank. I knew it was crap and I showed it anyway.

Why?

Because I was desperate!

Why?

My family is driving me crazy, especially my father.

Your father?

Yeah, doesn't everybody's father drive them crazy?

That's an understatement, she murmurs. About what?

That I'm a failure, that I picked the wrong field, that I am an embarrassment. But enough of that crap. Just come here. He takes off his shirt, slides out of his pants, his underwear, leans up on one elbow, pats the bed beside him, says, I miss you.

Rob stares at the rays of sunlight sending glints of copper through his dark hair, his long arms muscled like a swimmer's, slender legs, and thinks, Jesus Christ. Mick and Grace, they look alike, except for the cock, they look almost exactly alike. She laughs as she takes off her clothes, climbs into bed with him.

Something funny?

Not a thing. I missed you too. She nudges Benny with her foot, Move over big guy.

Mick reaches for her breast, does the things he has always done. She feels him licking, sucking, his long arms circling her back, pressing her tight against him and her body responds as it has always responded. She lets him clasp her neck, stare into her eyes, things she lets no one else do. And for the first time she wonders if this is just playing the game, like Danny said, how it is with Grace, or if this is what it is to love someone.

As he puts on his shoes he asks, Any wine left for me?

Nah, she says, slipping into Maria's faded chenille robe. It's all gone.

And your new work? Can I see it?

Not yet. It's not ready yet.

I need something, Rob. Need it soon.

You'll get it. I got a couple of ideas working, she lies.

Hey, did you ever finish that thing you were writing? You said you'd show me.

Nah, I threw that away, she lies again.

Aw fuck, I wanted to read it.

It wasn't anything, wasn't important.

I came home and saw a bunch of envelopes open on the kitchen table, everything inside ripped up—the responses to the college applications I had finally written away for. What the fuck, I yelled. Jonah? Why weren't you in school? I heard music coming from the basement. I stomped down the stairs. Half-way into the room, next to the water heater, Jonah hung from the chin-up bar, his broken neck ringed with a red stripe from the rope noose digging hard into his skin. Fly me to the moon, Let me play among the stars, Let me see what spring is like on A-Jupiter and Mars. Over and over. A tape loop. I don't know how long I stood by the stairs before I could cross the room. I knelt, tried, but couldn't look at his face so I wrapped my arms around his legs, laid my cheek against his thighs. Smelled his piss. Then I let him go, slowly, carefully, and turned up the volume. Fly Me To The Moon blared. No thinking. Only counting. I grabbed the money from the coffee can, tore open boxes until I found my duffle bag. Up in his room I stuffed every sketchbook, every drawing, every doodle in the bag. Pulled six World Books off the shelf before I got the one with her photos, yanked the portfolio from under the bed, shoved everything inside the bag. Took underwear, shirts, a couple pairs of jeans from my drawers. Grabbed the keys Coach believed he had hidden so well in the cabinet above the fridge, drove the station wagon to an empty lot, threw the keys in a garbage can, ran. At the train station I bought a one-way ticket. It wasn't crowded. I had two seats to myself. I held the duffel bag on my lap, like a baby, and stared at my reflection in the window, not thinking, not feeling, just counting the numbers in my head, until the train pulled into Penn Station.

She had a ton of names. Lola for the barflys, Jasmine for the pricy ones, Marcy for the cops when they came around for freebies, Alfie when she stuffed a sock down her pants and went down on women who like Butches. She never told me her real name. I never even found it out when they took her in the ambulance. She told me to call her Deborah, after Deborah

Kerr in that scene in From Here to Eternity. She took me to see it at the Bleecker Street Cinema. We used to act it out, pretend our crummy mattress was the beach, giggle about the tide coming in on our naked bodies. I called her Deborah out loud but in my mind she was Viola, from Twelfth Night, the boy/girl who figures out how to make it all work.

She found me sitting on a bench near the Hare Krishna tree in Tompkins Square Park. It was just two days after I got off the train and I was a total fucking mess. I had tried a couple of hotels near 42nd Street, but they wanted to see some ID. All I had was my driver's license showing I was seventeen. I wasn't sure you had to be older to get a room, so I ended up riding the subway the first night, me and a bunch of smelly men and women, all with duffels or strapped-together suit cases. If I wasn't so scared, tired, hungry and cold I would have laughed. I fit right in. Next night I found a crappy place on the Bowery, learned first-hand what a flea bag hotel was. I couldn't even stay all night, just left and headed uptown, ended up in the park.

She sat down next to me, stared at me for a really long time. She was dressed like a secretary, sort of. She had short, really short brown hair and wore a blue skirt and jacket, but also diamond patterned black stockings and very very blue high heels. She didn't say a word, just stared at me. Creeped me out.

I started to get up and she said, What's your name? Her voice was a jolt. She sounded just like Betty Boop. What's yours matey, I asked, doing a bad imitation of Popeye. She laughed and slapped me on the thigh. Got a cigarette? I wasn't smoking yet. Well then, you got any money to buy some? Not a whole lot. I gotta go to work now, she said, you got some place to go? You can't sleep here, this is my bench. You sleep here? She laughed, Kid, this is my office. Here. You. You go to 508 Avenue D, near the corner of D and 7th. The buzzer is broke, but just pound on the door. Somebody will let you in. Why? Because I told you, you can't sleep here.

I didn't want to go there, but it was freezing cold and where the hell else was I gonna go? Definitely not back to the crappy Bowery. It looked like all the benches in Tompkins Square Park were somebody's office. And I had been walking so long, the duffel bag getting heavier and heavier. The neighborhood got dirtier and dirtier the further I went toward the river, more and more men and women leaning on light poles, swaying. I stood in front of 508 for a long time. Some skanky guy came up the block, headed my way, so I banged on the door. After what seemed like forever the door opened. The guy who let me in didn't even look at me. He opened the door, turned and walked away. The place was dark, dank, doors on either side of a long hallway. It smelled like that boxwood shrub, like cat piss. There was a stairway, the railing busted out in places. I slammed the door shut, walked up the hallway. First room I passed was even darker, the only window covered with a saggy blanket. I couldn't even see in. Across the hall was a bigger room, lit by a single bulb in what was once a really fancy chandelier. I saw a few people, I couldn't be sure how many, laying on the floor, leaning up against the walls. I knew they were junkies, nodding out. I wasn't stupid. But they looked so peaceful, rested, that I zipped my coat up tight and just sank down in an empty space. I somehow fell asleep clutching my duffel bag and woke to someone poking me on the shoulder. I only recognized her by her voice. In a pair of tight jeans, black boots and white t-shirt she looked like a punk Peter Pan. She took me to the Binibon. Coffee is lousy but refills are free. Eggs pretty good. My treat. You gonna carry that bag everywhere? It's all...all I got. You want to go to work?

Hell, thanks to Teddy Ackroyd, I already knew how to give a blow job, but she taught me about the business. How to get the money up front, to keep an eye out for scabs or open sores, how to signal that I wasn't gonna fuck, just suck, where was the best place to go in the bushes, that I could sometimes get an extra five if I offered to swallow it, and then where to vomit once the guy was gone.

She negotiated an office for me in the park, I only

had to kick back one dollar a job to her and one to the previous tenant. For rent at 508 she did the guy who owned the squat twice a week, my rent was $50 a month and a once-a-week blow job. He was a jerk, but clean. Sometimes didn't even come to collect. I could never figure out who lived in the place. People came and went all day and all night. Deborah let me share her room on the top floor. It was the only room in the house with a window that opened onto the fire escape. She had a mattress with a box spring on the floor, a big scratched mirror on one wall, long rickety table with clothes, wigs, make-up on the other. Why am I nice to you? The only answer I ever got was something I know she'd heard in a movie, Because you remind me of someone.

I need to get out of here she said one day, not long after we got together. You wanna go to Far Rockaway? Not if it's a suburb. Nah, it's a beach. I've never seen the ocean. Not possible. Wanna bet?

End of the IRT. Beach 116th Street. You just get off the train, walk across a couple of streets and bam, a beach. I went there a few times after she was gone, in much nicer weather, even swam in the ocean once. We walked along the water, bundled up against the wind, sand in my eyes, my hair. That's it, she said. The Atlantic Ocean. Nothing between us and—Portugal, I said. Maybe northern Spain. You were good in school? Pretty good. Did you graduate? Where did you grow up, I asked. Right here. Nah! Yeah, not far from here.

We found one place open, a drafty wooden coffee shop. We were the only people in the place and it seemed the guy would have been just as happy if we hadn't shown up. You're pretty young to know what you know, she said. How did you get started? I told her about Teddy Ackroyd, how he had seen me and Danny, how he had me blow him in the dugout once every couple of weeks. Yeah, she said, I get it. You were afraid what your old man would do if he found out about you and that boy. Yeah, I said. But also because I wanted a bicycle. She looked at me. He gave me money so I could buy a bicycle. I started laughing, harder and harder, actually roaring until I was in tears, sobbing, and she was holding me. What's wrong with your friend, the guy asked, maybe you should go? She's sad, Deborah said. Sad about what? She never had a bike. She held my hand on the subway ride back.

We were good like that, for nearly a year. Fixed up the room, went shopping down in the lower East side for sheets and towels. Normal stuff, like we were a normal couple. We were sort-of-lovers because she mostly only wanted to cuddle, hold me. Enough with the sex stuff, she'd say as she smoked a joint. I get enough of that at the office. I didn't care. With Deborah it just really felt good to have a warm, friendly body next to me. Even with the junkies coming and going all over the house it was some of the best sleep I ever had.

After a night's work, we'd stay in bed until at least noon. Sometimes if there was hot water, take a bath together. If not, we washed each other's hair in the sink with water boiled on the hot plate. Then breakfast at Binibon. It wasn't so bad, the work. I got so I could get them off pretty quick. I was careful, never got any stds, and it was only that last time that anybody tried to hurt me.

One evening when I got to my bench there was this bird, a small dead bird, lying there. I started to kick it off, then for some reason just picked it up, held it in my hands. It was stiff, the feathers dry. But it was so light, so barely there. I held it for a long time, felt all along its body, tiny tiny bones. My hands liked it. I thought I ought to hate it, a stinking dead bird, but in my hands I felt like it belonged. I didn't want to lose that feeling. So when it was slow I would grab a branch off the ground, strip it and try to make it. I wanted to keep feeling it. It wasn't super dark, there were one or two lamp posts in the park that still worked, but if I had to, I could do it in the dark, by feel. Deborah said I would attract more business if I wasn't sitting there with an open knife, but we had plenty of money, were never hungry. The neighborhood got wilder, junkies came and went like newspapers blowing around the lamp-posts. They really weren't a problem in the house, when they were high they just nodded out. If they were jonesing they were out on the streets, robbing someone somewhere else. We talked about getting an actual apartment but never did anything about it.

You'd be surprised at the range of morons who sat down next to me. Lawyer-doctor types in suits and ties, scraggly-bearded hippies who looked like they couldn't scrape ten dollars together to go to their mother's funeral, creepy fat bald men with bad breath. Most of them didn't even look at me much, but they all wanted to hold my head, put their paws on either side of my temples, sometimes covering my ears. Which I learned to tolerate because in my mind I broke each and every finger, snapped it back till it popped. Open air blow jobs are at best an eight month proposition. When it got too cold to be outside I thought I would bring them to the house on Avenue D but Deborah said it was risky, me alone in the house with a trick. I thought about going full-on pro, work how she did, but Deborah said no, she didn't want me to. I'd have to audition for the pimp, she didn't want him to have me. It wasn't like I was broke, pretty much paid my share. So in the cold months, while she was sleeping in the mornings, I walked around the city. That's when I found Soho, found Mick's gallery. Must have looked in his window twenty times.

I don't know why she started using so much. She

was always smoking dope, but never shot up until that was all she was doing. This guy in the house, Frankie, slimy bastard, really handsy, kept giving her tastes until she was fully on. She had it under control, she said. As long as the money came in, the supply was good. She could handle it. The only time she was mean to me, got mad at me, was when I refused to try it, called me a chicken, a baby. So I did. Once. And holy mother of Christ on a crutch I totally got it. Everything, everything I was, my bones, my muscles, my skin, all turned to liquid, flowing liquid gold. My mind went somewhere—no thinking, no counting, no memories, nobody else inside me. A peace I had never felt, and have never felt since. I knew if I did it a second time, I would not stop, would never do anything else. Why would I want to feel anything except that sweetness. She was pretty far gone by that time, not working much anymore. Her dope habit was eating all my money. It wasn't her fault. There was some bad shit circulating, junkies od-ing in the streets, in the squats. I came back that evening and stood across the street out of range of the red swirling light, watched the medics carry her out the door. I'm getting sick of cleaning up this shit, one of them said. The other one told the driver as he opened the back of the ambulance, Don't bother with the siren. She's not gonna make it two blocks.

It took a few months until I ran out of money. I just

couldn't go back to the park. So I finally did it. I called the cops, told them about Frankie in 508 Avenue D. And the next day I went into Mick's gallery, showed him the birds. I don't think he believed that I actually made them, but I knew he wanted to fuck me. I was lucky.

The bowl is singing on Rob's palm, Benny's head rests on her thigh, his snores and the bowl's tones mixing. She watches Jasper, mimes him. Setting the mallet to the side, she raises the bowl to her mouth, the rim about an inch from her lips. Making no sound, just opening her mouth, thinking the sound wah-wah, the inside of her mouth changes shape, the bowl responds, the tones respond, rising, falling and slowly fading away. Jasper lowers his hands. Rob lays the bowl in her lap.

Wow wow wow wow wow, Rob whispers.

No, wah-wah, he says.

You've got the sense of humor of a six year-old. Why does it work? How the hell does that work?

He shrugs. Vibration, all about the vibrations. You want to try another way?

Are you kidding?

He sets the bowl on her palm, pours a little water into the bottom. You have to be careful, he says, not to get any water on the outside. Here, he hands her the mallet. Just play it like you always do.

She sets the bowl singing, he mimes pulling the mallet away, tilting the bowl. She does as he does and the tones are higher, become almost shrill.

Rob drops the mallet, lowers the bowl nearly spilling the water. She said it was dolphins singing. When she cried, that it was like dolphins singing.

She?

Rob shakes her head. Not important. So I got this.

Right? I'm ready to get one of my own? Finally? Where do I get one?

Jasper looks into her eyes, puts a hand on her shoulder. Yes, you got this, as you put it. But you have to know that when you play the bowl your body will absorb the vibrations you set up. Vibrations are energy and too much energy is not good, for anybody. It can actually make you sick. The stronger the vibration you set up, the harder it can hit you.

Nah! It feels good!

In the beginning, yes, but your body will have to do something with the energy that you create.

She pushes Benny off her lap, stands up, says in a mock professorial tone, Energy can neither be created nor ....

Don't be an ass! Yeah, you are good with this. Got a great touch. But it's not something to play with.

You think I'm playing?

Not playing playing. Just not understanding how serious.

Hey, I brought you something.

She hands him a small cardboard box, the top flaps ripped off. One of her clay bird bowls sits in a nest of crumpled waxed paper. He takes it out carefully, sets it on his palm.

You made this?

What, you think I stole it?

He looks deeply in her eyes, Robin, it's wonderful, truly wonderful.

She drops her eyes, lets out a breath. So where can I get one, she asks, pointing to the bowl on the cushion.

He sets the bowl she has been using on a purple silk scarf, adds the mallet, ties the ends of the scarf together, extends it to her.

Really?

It's one I've had it for years.

She holds it against her chest, fearful of dropping it. Damn. Jasper.

I know. It's always been yours. Just be careful, please.

Grace folds her coat carefully, sets it on a wooden chair, the least likely place to accumulate dog hair. This is beautiful, she says, taking up the singing bowl from the kitchen table. Where did you get it?

Rob turns from the sink, wipes the dishwater off her hands on her t-shirt. Was a gift, she says. From Jasper, my meditation teacher.

It looks genuine. Really old. He just gave it to you?

We traded. I gave him a sculpture.

You just gave him a sculpture? Honey, you can't just give your work away!

Why not? It's mine. Besides it was just a little one, a little bird.

Still. You have a reputation now, a track record.

I'm not running the 440 here. She takes the bowl

from Grace's hands. Have you ever used one? Heard it played?

Once. At a conference. How long have you been meditating?

A few months. It helps—

With?

Getting ideas, she lies. You know, she makes air quotes, "the whole creative process."

Will you play it for me?

Yeah, OK. Sure, why not. She motions to the bed, Best to climb up, it's more comfortable there.

Benny leaps up after Rob, nestles next to her.

What about the dog?

What about the dog? You mean the sounds? He loves them. Puts him right to sleep. Are you in or out?

Grace sits cross-legged on the bed, facing Rob, knees almost touching. Benny lays his head on Rob's lap.

You've done the meditation breathing thing?

Grace nods.

Jasper usually gives me something to visualize.

Like?

Like remember yourself as a child.

Grace nods again, That's fine.

They breathe for a few minutes, easily falling into unison. After a bit, Rob strikes the bowl, allows the tones to ring, then sends the mallet slowly around the rim. Benny grunts, settles in deeper. She thinks, maybe this time, maybe this time she'll be there. She lets the tones weave her, waiting for the voices. Grace inhales sharply, and Rob senses a change in her, wonders if she should stop but she keeps playing the bowl, caught up in her own desires.

Benny stirs, Grace moans, then yells No! The mallet falls from Rob's hand, she clutches the bowl, the tones silenced. She opens her eyes to see Grace sobbing.

Benny shifts so that his head rests against Grace's thigh. She pushes him away, wipes her nose with her sleeve.

Rob sets the bowl aside, takes Grace's hand. What happened? Did you—

Grace pulls her hand from Rob's, sits on the edge of the bed. It was like I was there, she says, when I was a kid. My grandmother, locking me in the closet, leaving me for hours. Never knowing for how long. She thought she was protecting me from the Nazis. I spent years dealing with that, in and out of therapy. I don't let it have much of an impact any more. At least I thought I didn't.

Yeah. I've had times like that. With the bowl.

And you like it? What happens?

I don't know. Rob climbs next to her. I don't have a fucking clue what happens. I don't see anything. It's just feelings. Sensations.

This kind of thing happened to you before?

Sometimes. Jasper says I must be introspective, maybe empathetic.

I love you honey but those are not the first words that come to mind.

That's what I said! But I can usually block it out. If I want.

What do you do?

Rob jumps off the bed, Benny follows. Hey, how about some dinner? I could make—

Tell me. What are you blocking out?

Nothing! I don't know! I just count. In my head. Numbers. Over and over. And it goes away. It's no big deal—

Possibly not, but—

Can we do this some other time? Like maybe never?

Why? I can help—

I don't want you to!

Grace bends to put on her shoes. It's alright. I understand.

Don't say you do when you don't.

I can help, Rob. For real.

Yeah but then you're different. To me. We become different. I want this to be the same. Come on. I'll go with you, help you find a cab. I need to walk Benny anyway.

It's up to you, Grace says. But I'd like to talk about this more.

As she grabs Benny's leash Rob thinks, I'll bet you do.

Rob gingerly pulls the plastic tarp off the piece she's been working on. The face stares back at her, tranquil, stoic, like the wife of a Roman emperor.

Not right, not right, she says, then yells, Son of a bitch! Fuck it. Just fuck it.

She grabs a wooden modeling tool, stands square to the head, then tosses it aside and uses her fingers to force the beautifully formed mouth open into a scream, scrapes a scar down one cheek with her fingernails. Benny whines, heads for the tiny space between the bathtub and the wall.

Aw crap. Benny! I'm sorry. Again. I'm sorry. She coaxes him out, kneels, presses her head against his forehead.

She sits cross legged on the bed, the bowl in her lap, mallet beside her. Now calm, Benny lies beside her. She breathes, just like Jasper taught her, feels that quiet, that heaviness she has come to crave. Remember, she says to herself, remember yourself as a child. Taking up the bowl and mallet, she sets the bowl singing.

Jesus Robin, Coach yells. easy, just swing it easy. you're too small to power it, you have to let the bat do the work for you. just get your hips into it and connect with the fat part. Robin says, it's heavy. of course it's heavy, he says, it's made of hickory, this one is old hickory. Jonah asks, like Andrew Jackson? what the hell does that have to do with baseball? I learned in school. it was his nickname, Old Hickory. Coach snarls, he was a bastard. Jonah is amazed. you knew him? don't be an idiot. so why a bastard? he sent Indians on The Trail of Tears. we look at Coach blankly. he sent all the Indians west, stole their land. don't you learn anything in school? they told us he was a war hero. how do you know about the Trail of Tears? a Cherokee guy I knew in the army. it happened to his grandparents. you were in the army? don't be a moron! who wasn't in the damned army!

Not him again! she yells, throwing the mallet across the room. It's supposed to be her! I don't want him in my head!

She lays next to Benny, wraps her arms and legs around him to stop him from jumping off the bed. Sorry Benny, she whispers, sorry. I'm trying. She feels his heartbeat slow as they both relax. Then she shoves herself off the bed, approaches the head of the woman, finds a wooden scraper and carefully, slowly, re-forms the mouth, repairs the cheek. The clay face stares back, once again tranquil, stoic.

Jasper, I need help. It's not working.

He takes the bowl from her palm, inspects the inside, the bottom. It looks fine, he says. And you've gotten better, you still have that nice touch, the mallet sits well in your hand.

But I'm not getting what I want.

This is getting old Rob. The bowl will sing when it's stroked. It doesn't care who plays it. It gives the same thing to everybody. Don't blame the bowl for what you are finding.

I'm looking for something—

What you are looking for is what you are finding. The bowl harmonizes with whatever is inside you.

Maybe if you do it, maybe if you make it sing and I just meditate. Like that first time?

You're turning this into some kind of parlor trick, some magical thinking bullshit. This is just a tool—

She grabs the bowl and mallet, shoves them in her bag. Fuck you you moron! Why won't you help me?

Jasper rises from his cushion, says quietly, You need to go. Now.

Rob struggles to her feet, shoulders her bag roughly, stops and looks at Jasper with tears in her eyes. I don't mean to, it just happens. I didn't mean—

You are welcome to come back. Another time.

At the door he says, Take the stairs, I need the elevator. Maybe it will burn off some of that energy. And stop using the bowl so often.

You should have seen it, Seymour.

Seymour clips hair off Benny's shoulder, close to his hide, wipes the small cut with warm water and a clean rag. He takes a pinch of powder from a battered tin, holds it on the wound. In a minute or two the bleeding stops.

Rob paces across the kitchen. It was this guy, she says, he came out of nowhere, over on Spring Street. Out from behind a dumpster. Not a junkie. A big guy. No sound, no warning. I didn't even see the knife.

Seymour runs his hands gently down Benny's back, scratches under his chin. Benny's eyes slowly close, his body relaxes.

He jumped, in front of me. Benny did. Jumped right at the guy. No barking, no growling. Just jumped so hard it pulled the leash out of my hand. He went for the guy's throat, the guy swiped at him, Benny yelped. I guess that's when he got cut. But he kept going. Trying to hurt the guy.

Of course he did.

He knocked the guy sideways, jumped on his chest. I pulled him off and we ran. I didn't notice the bleeding until we got to the door.

the girl slams the much larger boy against the locker. leave my brother alone! the big kid scoffs, how can such a wimp be Coach's kid? she grabs Jonah's arm, walks him backwards. just fuck off, all of you, fuck off. the big boy lunges at her. the girl raises her arm, shoots out her fingers and pokes him in the eye. he recoils, shrieks, covers his face. you got it? she says. all of you, fuck off.

It'll be OK, Seymour helps Rob lift Benny up onto the bed. It's not so deep.

Rob climbs up, lays behind Benny, one arm across his belly. I'm sorry, buddy, she whispers, I should have seen it, should have stopped it.

Nah, it's alright, Seymour says, it's his job. You gotta let him do his job. He lays the tin on the kitchen table. It's just alum, won't hurt him. Put more on if it bleeds again. Don't walk so much for a couple of days.

Seymour. Jesus. You're always around. I owe you. How can I—

You don't owe. I like dogs. And you're the only one ever wanted to learn about the elevator.

You're getting to be a habit, Grace says as she strokes Rob's naked back.

A good one or a bad one?

A good one. Mostly.

On a scale of one to ten?

Grace swings her feet off the bed, puts on a pair of wool socks before she steps onto the cold floor. It's May already for god's sake, does it ever warm up in here? I can't keep coming down here. I still don't see why you don't move up to—

Come back in August, Rob says. So I'm guessing that's a 3?

Grace sighs. Way more than a 3. But you're a huge distraction. I'm neglecting my work. I actually missed an appointment last week. And I have a workshop coming up at The New School. I've been down here almost every night. I need—

You need?

Space. Time.

As in the continuum or as in actuality.

Puck—

You can't call me that.

Are you still meditating?

Tell me about The New School.

Rob, it's really annoying—

The New School is annoying?

For Christ's sake!

On the Anger scale, was that a 3 or a 4?

What the hell?

I'm sorry I'm such a, she strikes a pose, distraction.

You really are a kid, Grace mutters.

Old enough to fuck though, huh?

Why are you doing this?

This? Getting dressed?

I don't have time for this shit, Grace grabs her coat, heads for the door.

Rob watches, makes it up to a count of six then follows her. Crap! I'm sorry! It's not you. She yanks the plastic tarp from the clay head, tosses it on the floor. This. This is what's driving me crazy.

Benny runs up to the tarp, stomps on it, barks.

Sorry, B, Rob says, patting his head.

Grace stops, stares at the face. She plops down on an upturned metal bucket, says, But it's stunning. What are you mad at? It looks exactly like her.

But it's NOT her! Or it's too much her! I have no fucking idea.

Grace walks behind Rob, reaches up, begins to massage her neck.

Rob freezes, whispers, Not my neck.

What? Grace backs away. Why?

Rob turns, her arms loose at her sides, head bowed. I'm sorry, she says, Long story.

Grace opens her arms, I have time.

Except that you don't. You just said.

Hey. Rob, Grace says softly. Come to this workshop I'm giving. On Saturday. It's a one-time thing. Just a couple of hours.

Rob stands up straight, shakes her head, I don't know from school, new or otherwise. Academics don't—

It won't be academic. It's just a group of women exploring ways to deal with anger. We'll be doing Experiential Psych exercises.

Whatever the fuck that is.

You'll love it. Trust me.

Rob is late. She hung around on West 12th Street for twenty minutes, smoking, not sure she wanted to see Grace-as-teacher. Or see herself as student-of-Grace. But she stands near the classroom door, watching her in front of the room reading from a dog-eared copy of *Poems of Rumi*. She had expected a straight-backed full of authority, no-nonsense Grace. This is a different Grace altogether—kinder, softer than Rob had ever seen her. The other women in the class, all eight of them, are reading along on the hand-out. Except for a few of them being short, some taller, long hair, short hair, the women are somehow alike, like members of a Greek chorus. Rob is the outlier, at least fifteen years younger, wearing a battered jeans jacket and stained, painted boots instead of expensive loafers.

Grace finishes the poem, scans the class, smiling when she spots Rob. So, she says, the poet is telling us that we should accept all that comes at us, not as problems but as opportunities. And we should be grateful for those opportunities. Every moment is important and every day has something to teach us. As Rumi says, *This being human is a guest house. Every morning a new arrival.*

A tiny woman in the front pipes up, So when my husband pisses me off I'm supposed to think it's "clearing me out for some new delight?"

Yeah, are we supposed to "treat him honorably?

Grace laughs, It's not about what other people are doing to you but what you feel about it, how you respond. The guests are you, your feelings, the good ones and the bad ones. We need to learn to welcome them all.

I'd rather forget about them. Why the hell would I want to welcome bad feelings?

Rob thinks, Because they are fucking going to happen, then mutters "For sweetest things turn sourest by their deeds; Lilies that fester smell far worse than weeds."

Grace nods, points to Rob, Wise words from the peanut gallery.

Rob smiles, takes a seat in the back of the room.

Tiny woman begins, I get mad, and the chorus adds, Killer mad. But I keep it inside, stuff it down. I'm afraid of what I'll do. If I start, I don't know if I'd ever stop. Sometimes all I want to do is scream.

Unfortunately none of those responses are unusual, Grace says. But you've hit on a good one. Screaming is actually a useful tool to get the anger out of your body. How about we all scream?

The women glance at each other, laugh nervously.

Really?

Grace nods, Really. Stand up. Think of someone you want to scream at, have always wanted to scream at. Visualize them sitting in your chair. Let 'er rip.

Just scream?

Scream, yell, talk loud. Give them the finger. Say everything you've always wanted to say.

One by one the women turn to face their chairs. Rob watches.

Arrrrhhhghhh! One tall woman half-yells, pointing at her empty chair.

We've got a pirate, Rob thinks.

Good, good, Grace encourages. More. Louder. Come on, all of you.

The chorus responds. Screams, screeches, undifferentiated shouts. Laughter.

After several minutes the tiny woman kicks over her chair, yells at the top of her lungs, I hate you! I want to kill you!

The women fall silent, step back from their chairs, look at anything but each other.

I know you do, Grace says softly. But you won't. Wanting is not the same as doing. Acknowledging, verbalizing, feeling that hate, that rage, having it outside of you is a good thing. A healthy thing.

I wish she had run the Anger Management course, Rob thinks, it would have been a lot more fun.

Grace rights the overturned chair. Thanks, Margot, for the great segue. All right. Time to tap your imagination. Everyone put somebody in the chair, somebody you have always wanted to say something to but never did, for whatever reason. We're not here to delve too deep. That would take a long time and we've only got a few hours. I don't care about the reason you are angry, what has caused your pain, why you have been unable to confront it. I just want you to face that person and say what you've always wanted to say. No screaming now, find the words.

They are into it now. Grace moves the chairs apart, giving each woman more room, a wider space. Little by little they start talking.

You son of a bitch! How many times do you think I'll take you back! Ma! You always side with her! I AM so capable of writing that report! Why don't you ever give me a chance?

Rob slouches before an empty chair, listening to the women rail against their demon, their mother, their whatever. She tunes them out, is sure she will see Coach, spew vitriol, stunted feelings, if not aloud, at least in her mind. But all she sees in the chair is a beautiful boy. Jonah. His goofy laugh, crooked teeth, constant annoying, wondering questions. His humor, his gentle, gentle spirit. Shocked by the memory, she finds herself reciting the twenty-ninth sonnet.

When, in disgrace with fortune and men's eyes,
I all alone beweep my outcast state
And trouble deaf heaven with my bootless cries
And look upon myself and curse my fate,
Wishing me like to one more rich in hope,
Featured like him, like him with friends possess'd,
Desiring this man's art and that man's scope,
With what I most enjoy contented least; Yet in these
thoughts myself almost despising,

Haply I think on thee, and then my state,
Like to the lark at break of day arising
From sullen earth, sings hymns at heaven's gate;
For thy sweet love remembered such wealth brings
That then I scorn to change my state with kings.

Only Grace notices, hears Rob. She longs to find out, ask who is in that chair, who is the fair-haired young man she loves so deeply. But the other women have yelled themselves out. They are flushed, a little confused but happy, vindicated.

Let's take ten, Grace says. Coffee in the lounge. Be back at 2:30.

Grace starts toward Rob but she slips out the door, down to the street. Her hands are shaking as she lights a smoke. Enough of this shit, she thinks as she heads east on 12th, stops at the corner and turns back. Grace, she says to herself, you would have liked Jonah.

The chairs are still spread around the room. The women finish their coffee, toss empty cups in the trash.

Okay, Grace says, Here we go. Last exercise of the day. Grab those pillows, the big ones, and put them on your chair.

Rob hangs back, watches as the women stuff the pillows onto the chairs. The sadness brought on by remembering Jonah numbs her.

We've done good work today, Grace says. Looked at

the fact that we aren't expressing ourselves. Found a tool to voice our anger. Really good work. Hard work.

She points to a row of scratched, yellow whiffle-ball bats standing in the corner of the room.

Now we up the ante, she says as she picks up a bat. Gain another tool to physically express our anger, a way to get it outside our bodies, Anybody up for some base-ball?

Yeah! I get it, the tiny woman yells and grabs a bat, slams the pillow on her chair. Hits it on the side, from the top, over and over until she is exhausted.

Grace laughs, takes the bat from her. That's it! Let it out. How did that feel?

The tiny woman nods, over and over, says breathless-ly, I could do that every single day!

Rob's eyes go wide. In an instant the sadness lifts and it clicks. She shoves her arms into her jacket says, Whoa, sorry. I gotta go!

Grace says, Wait! What?

All good, Rob yells over her shoulder. All fucking good!

So this is it? Mick yells. The big surprise? You're kid-ding, yes?

Rob has spent the last three weeks in a frenzy. No Grace, no Mick, no singing bowl, not as much booze. Just working. Ripped magazines litter the floor of her studio.

Faces cut from ads are pinned to the wall boards—women in haute couture clothes, smiling couples in expensive restaurants, men showing off their Patek Philippe watches. Four life-sized heads of models from the ads are set on individual pedestals in the center of the floor. Sculpted from Plastilina, the grey-green heads are perfect, like the faces in the ads are perfect. Symmetrical, slim, classic Greek statues.

So really? This is it? Mick says again. Are you kidding me? A bunch of heads? They are beautiful. You get an A in art but who wants, he picks up a block of clay, chucks it across the room, a head made of Plastilina for Christ's sake!

Woah! Wait! Let me show you—

And you can't use model's faces—

I know!

It doesn't cure. You can't fire it.

Exactly! That's the kicker. You are gonna love this. Total audience participation. A logical extension of *Disfigure*. Gimme a sec, let me take Benny down to Seymour, he gets really upset.

Seymour gets upset?

No, Benny! You'll see. Just wait.

OK, she says, after running up the stairs, Watch. She picks up a wooden baseball bat, squares up to one of the heads, like she is waiting for a pitch to come across the plate. Mick steps away, holds his hands in front of his chest.

No, no, not that, Rob says as she swings for all she's worth into the side of the head of the beautiful perfume model. No catching this one, she says, this is a home fucking run.

The ear collapses. She hits it again, this time with an upswing, like she is playing golf. The wood connects with a loud slap, the chin driven up against the metal armature inside. She gets ready to swing again.

Stop! Mick covers his ears with his hands. What the fuck! It sounds like a watermelon dropped from the roof. Why would anybody want that?

Trust me. I spent a whole Saturday with a bunch of women who paid real money to bash a pillow that was supposed to be somebody they hated. They aren't psycho killers, just really really angry and they don't know what to do with themselves. Don't know how to let it out. Never even yelled in their entire lives much less hit anything. There are a fucking lot of very angry people in this town. With money. I can give them something to take it out on. They bring me some photos, I make some sketches, then sculpt the head. They take it home and do whatever the hell they want with it. Hit it with a hammer, a bat, stick a knife in it, throw it out the window. I don't care! It only takes a couple of days to make one, the material is dirt cheap.

How can you be fine with people destroying your work?

Destroying it IS the work! This will be huge! Steven-

son will call it a statement about the prevalence of re-
pressed anger in modern culture or some shit like that.
You gotta see that, Mick.

He shakes his head, I don't know Robbie.

She thrusts the bat into his hands, Try it. Just try it.
Who are you mad at? Really mad at?

Other than you?

Ha ha. I mean it. Just see one of these heads as someone you've always wanted to—

Joey Doolin from fifth grade.

Why him?

An asshole bully, never left me alone. Still hate the
little fucker.

So let him have it.

Mick takes the bat, raises it, like a sword, and lets
it fall onto the top of one of the heads. Barely makes a
dent.

Rob sneers. That's it? That's how much you hate him?

Mick adjusts his grip, raises it again, high over his
head, and smashes down. He grunts. Turns sideways,
lifts the bat again, slams it straight across the face. Nose
and eyes smashed beyond recognition. He bashes the
head, over and over, grunting with each blow, leaving
a mutilated mass of green clay lying next to the metal
armature. He flings the bat across the room, eyes glazed
like a B-movie villain and lunges at Rob. She pushes him
aside, sends him crashing into a pile of tarps.

Mick looks back at the head, holds his hands in front

of him, stares at Rob. I have never hit anything either, he says, in my entire life, I have never hit one single thing. Why did it feel like that?

Like?

Good! It was such a turn on! And horrible! I don't know what the hell to feel. It felt so right when I was doing it—

You never played a sport? Wrestled with your brother?

He shakes his head. Only child. And an arty kid. Jocks were Neanderthals. Jesus. I never knew what that felt like. Sexy and bad, sexy and good. Did you? Hit things? Play sports?

Long story, she says to herself.

And Robbie. Jesus, about that ... I don't know why I did that—

I do, she says quietly. Don't worry. She crosses the room, picks up the bat, stands it next to her workbench. Mick, what's this about. What are we doing?

Hopefully making each other rich and famous--

No, I mean why. Why did you help me? Why do you still?

I liked you, liked your little birds—

She shoots him the side eye.

Yeah alright. At first I just wanted to fuck you. You have one of those bodies, like you were born to be fucked. Your style, energy is so different—

From all the Jonis.

He stares at her, laughs. Yeah, I guess they do all look alike.

So that was at first. Now?

Why you asking? Now?

Don't know. Just feeling—

You got under my skin, kiddo. Like a little sister or something. What am I, fifteen years older? And you drive me crazy. But you are an amazing artist, Robbie. I don't know much about much else, but I do know talent when I see it. I can't imagine anyone else thinking up this head thing. It could be huge. For both of us.

She waits. For something else, anything more.

And, hey. I really did like your little birds.

She gives up. So about the show—

Hell yes. I get it. I'm in. Let me talk to a few people, figure out how it would work in the gallery.

She turns away, pours a drink. So make more?

It's already April. Can you be ready by September?

Not a problem.

Got a title?

This one is easy. *Restitution.*

How about Hitler? Nixon?

What the fuck? Rob tosses her cigarette into the gutter, turns to Mick, who the hell is this?

Melanie, Rob, Rob, Melanie.

Good Christ, Rob thinks, a Joni with big boobs and frizzy hair?

I hired her, Mick says, to do PR for the show. She's brilliant. We've figured out how to keep control of the idea, how to get the word out about commissions, now we need to decide on what head you should beat on at the opening.

I'm not looking for ideas here, Rob says.

Melanie leans forward, puts her hand on Rob's arm. But I can get more people here if—

Rob shakes off her hand, turns to Mick. I'm not sculpting hitlers. Or serial killers. Or politicians or celebrities. I'll give you a head. Just let me do what I do.

Secret, Melanie says, nodding. OK. Mystery. I can work with that. But are you sure you don't want to—

Rob waves them off over her shoulder, heads into her building.

She does what she always does. Takes Benny and walks—across town, uptown, downtown. Grace has gone to Europe for some conference, Mick and Melanie are busy making plans for her September opening. She has no fear that she will be ready, she knows she can make a head in a couple of days. But each time she stands at the workbench, the metal armature rod set firmly into the wooden base, the ball of clay in her hands—nothing. She was sure she would see Coach in the mass of green/gray, easily find his features, that sneering, hateful expression. But her hands won't move, fingers stay curled around the ball of clay. Not even the Singing Bowl helps. She has played it, at least once each day for several weeks, and nothing. No voice she wants to hear, no voice she is afraid to hear.

You're not going to let me see?

Rob secures the plastic sheet over the sculpture. Mick, I'll bring it to the gallery, she says, Seymour will help with the hand truck. It's just a couple of blocks.

So you showed him? Not me?

Jesus. Give it up. I haven't showed anybody. Nobody has seen it but me.

Yeah good. It's going to be huge. Melanie killed with the publicity. She even got Stevenson to come back.

Oh joy. Just make sure the pedestal is set up. And bring the bat. I'll be there by five.

That's cutting it close. We open at—

Will you leave me the fuck alone!

He rests his hands on her shoulders, looks into her eyes. Robbie, you're good, yes? This is a big night—

She shrugs him off, I'll be there.

When he is gone she takes the singing bowl and mallet, sits in the center of the bed. Breathes in, breathes out. Plays the bowl. Hears the tones, falls into them. Praying, hoping for her voice, for some proof that she is not alone. The tones swirl, take her up, around, but the voices are silent.

Nothing, she mutters to Benny. Could have been worse, could have gotten him. She slides off the bed, pats the dog. Wish me luck, Benvolio. You stay here tonight. Too much pounding gonna happen. Outside her loft she bangs on the pipe to let Seymour know to send up the elevator, then packs the sculpture in a wooden crate.

Nearly a hundred people mill around in front of the gallery. Melanie is truly no slouch in the PR department. Reps from the art mags, area papers, and, of course, Geoffrey Stevenson, mingle with artists, clients, all eager to see what was promised to be a revolutionary leap in art making and collecting. Rob pushes past the crowd, sets the veiled sculpture on the waiting pedestal, then goes into the office to change her clothes. Grace helps her into a black leather shirt she brought back from Milan, squeezes her shoulders.

Oh now that is sexy! You look amazing! And here, I know these will be perfect for you.

just put this on her mother says. for me? don't you want to look pretty? the girl holds up her arms, the pink taffeta dress falls over her shoulders, fits tight to her waist. the girl squirms, tries to pull her body away from the stiff fabric. stay still, her mother says, and this, we'll put this bow in your hair. now you're pretty.

Rob runs her hands awkwardly down the pair of pants made entirely of industrial-sized zippers. I don't know Grace, she says, the top of me feels like a cow. And you're sure these will stay zipped?

Relax. Sweetheart. You finally look the part! My art star! I told all my friends, colleagues. I can't wait to see what you've done! Come out, I'll get you a glass of wine.

Are you going to throw anything at me this time?

Rob spins, nearly bumps into Stevenson, laughs a nervous laugh. That was so dumb, she says. You were totally right. I get it—that I have to be able to say what I'm doing even if don't know what I'm doing until after I've done it.

He nods his smug balding head. And tonight? What can you tell me about this work?

Excuse me, Geoffrey, it is really great to see you, Mick butts in, but we have to get started. He takes Rob by the elbow, steers her into the center of the room says, Time, kiddo. You're on.

Melanie and the new Joni shoo people away from the pedestal. Mick raises his glass to the crowd saying, Thank you, thank you all for coming tonight. I am thrilled to present this body of work. Rob Morgan, who I'm sure you remember from *Disfigure,* is taking the idea of viewer participation to an entirely new and powerful level. This work not only allows you to be part of the process, it gives you equal control in the creation of the piece, will afford you a means to express yourself, even come to terms with people in your life. Morgan's work is extremely personal and completely universal. Rob?

Rob squares her shoulders, walks to the pedestal. She slowly unclips the plastic covering, folds it neatly, hands it to Melanie and reveals the face of a larger than life-size, beautifully rendered middle-aged man, his head slightly cocked to the left, chin up, mouth slack, eyes half-open in a stupor. A perfect depiction of Teddy Ackroyd getting a blow job.

Rob scans the crowd, looks directly at Grace, says, Here is the head of someone I am very angry at. Anger that has defined a part of my life. Tonight I will get rid of that anger, take control of my life. Tonight I will get restitution.

Mick hands her the bat. Murmurs from the crowd. She makes a full circuit of the pedestal then squares up to the sculpture and swings for the fences. The left side of Teddy's cheek collapses against the armature.

A collective gasp, then silence.

Rob pulls back the bat, just like Coach taught her, re-takes her strong stance, lifts her left leg from the knee, stomps down and swings again. And again. Direct hits. There is little left of Teddy's face.

My God! somebody screams.

From behind, Rob pounds the head, three solid strokes.

A tall woman, dressed in a flowing red dress pushes her way toward the pedestal. I get it! she cries. I get it! I want five!

Five? Mick asks. A five-headed—

Five! One for each year I was married to the bastard! Where do I sign?

Silence followed by laughter.

I get it, I get it too, a short man yells. I know just who I want you to make.

Rob stands tall, takes a last swing at Teddy's head, smashes those glazed-over eyes closed for good. She rests the bat carefully against the pedestal, raises her arms, steps back from the mutilated head. A couple of cheers, a few people clap, then the entire room erupts into loud and long applause. Melanie pokes Mick with her elbow, holds out the price list, points a finger up to the ceiling. He smiles.

Viewers crowd around the pedestal. The questions come fast and furious.

What, it's some kind of clay?

Did you HEAR that sound?

I wouldn't use a bat, maybe throw darts?

Can you re-make it once it's beat up?

Rob looks around for Grace, sees that she's gone out on the street. She notices Stevenson heading her way and ducks out.

She smiles at Grace, So?

Grace looks sick, whispers. I can't believe you did that. How could you do that?

Did what? Do what?

Hit that face like that. Smash that face—

It was your idea! I got it from you, from the work-shop.

The pillow thing? That was not a face!

You told her to do it! To let it out! It was a woman swinging a bat at someone she hated.

But that was just symbolic!

So you're good with beating up a symbol but not a sculpture of the person that the symbol comes from? It's a clay head for Christ's sake, not a real person! What the fuck?

It looked so real. Like an actual person. And you were so into it. So violent. How could you be so violent?

You haven't got the least fucking inkling about violent! You think THAT was violent? What about what he did? You don't even care why I picked him?

How could I care? You never tell me anything!

That's because my business is my business. Nothing in my life is yours. It's none of your business!

Grace's head snaps back, as if she had been slapped. Yeah, I know that. Now. You never said one single thing about your life. You know may a lot about violence but you don't have the least fucking inkling about intimacy!

Rob reaches out, then steps back, lets her arms fall to her sides. She sneers and says, Go, will ya? You're just gonna leave anyway.

It's just too much. I can't, just can't. This part of town, the dog...

I don't need reasons. So I'm guessing this means the hurlyburly's done?

Grace sighs, smiles, Such a great memory. I'm sorry, Rob. I tried. We're just too—I think I'm just shakespeared out.

Rob watches Grace turn and head up the sidewalk, arm raised, hailing a cab. She waits to feel the pain, the usual boiling anger at being rejected. But there is only relief, mixed with a small sorrow, and she realizes that all she wants to do is get out of the leather shirt, take off the stupid zipper pants. She takes a deep breath, gets ready to meet Mick, talk to Stevenson, even willing to meet the buyers. But before she can head back to the gallery a hand reaches from behind her, taps her lightly on the shoulder. Not now, she says and turns to swat it away.

No fucking way, she whispers. Danny?

Hey Puck.

In the last few years his face and chest have filled out, he's maybe put on ten pounds. In a good way. His blonde hair, which had always been short, is long, thick, brushed straight back from his forehead, falling onto his shoulders. He wears the hippie uniform—black T-shirt under jeans jacket, faded bellbottoms, pointy leather boots and the ubiquitous Guatemalan woven cotton backpack slung over his shoulder.

Are you alone? Is he?

No no. Just me.

Rob catches her breath, lets out a sob.

Oh fuck, he blurts. I'll go.

No, god no. It's just, she gestures to Grace heading down the block, to Mick obviously searching for her in the gallery. Come on, she says. Let's get out of here.

You can?

Hell, she wipes her nose on the Italian leather shirt, I'm the art star.

Rob pulls back the gate on the elevator she helped fix, bangs once on Seymour's door, yells, Taking it up!

This is where you live? Danny asks.

So?

It's cool!

They ride up in silence, do an awkward dance as she unlocks the three deadbolts on the door of the loft.

Oh man, Danny yells when she flips on the lights. This is your place?

A sublet, I'm just here till the owners get back. Jesus, Danny. It's such a long story, everything is gonna be such a long story.

Benny rushes up from the back, stops cold, stands and stares at Danny, doesn't bark, doesn't growl.

Whoa, he's a beaut! Can I pet him?

Up to him.

Danny kneels on the floor, holds out one hand, waits. Benny watches, then pads calmly forward, shoves his snout under Danny's hand.

What a beautiful dog, he whispers. Where did you?

He found me.

Is he a Groenendael?

How does everybody know that?

Benny relaxes fully under his hands. I always wanted a big dog. My father would only get annoying stupid beagles. I can't believe this place! Look at all this cool stuff. What do you do with those hoses —

Later, I'll show you later. I need a drink. She leads him to the back of the loft, parts the curtain.

Wow! It's like walking onto a stage.

Yeah, I am really lucky. She uncorks the last bottle of Grace's wine, pours some into the bent metal cups. Do you?

Sure, he takes the cup, starts to sit at the table.

I have to get changed.

Oh no! he mugs. I love that outfit.

She cracks up, is on the verge of tears again. Hey, here. Opening the back window she props it up with the stick, tells him, Go on up. I'll be there in a sec.

She watches him climb easily out the window, his steps loud on the metal stairs, smiles when she hears him yell Wow! when he gets to the top. She sheds Grace's clothes, throws on a turtleneck and overalls, then sprints to the door of the loft, feels her hand on the locks, sees herself running down the street. What was that shit about cowards and death, she mutters, and turns back. Benny settles down on the bed.

Rob straddles the milk crate, puts the bottle of wine on the table, asks, How the hell did you find me?

I came looking a couple of times before, once pretty soon after you'd left and once about a year ago, remembered you said you had lived on West Tenth Street.

Yeah?

There's a lot of West Tenth Street. Coach said some shit about you moving to Ohio or something. Some aunt or something.

Ohio? An aunt?

Yeah, right? He was different after you left. We barely talked to each other. No way was I going to find you.

So how did you?

There was a notice. In Rolling Stone. About the exhibit. Called you Rob Morgan.

For real? You read Rolling Stone? And you came to New York just because of that?

I wanted to see if it was you.

Is it?

I'd know that swing anywhere.

Rob takes a long gulp of wine. Is he?

Still there.

Team still winning?

Why did you leave? We were right there, ready to graduate. You could have—

I couldn't.

He sets his cup on the table, closes his eyes, whispers, And you couldn't call?

I tried. Tons of times.

Yeah?

After a while it got too hard. How could I even start?

That's fucking lame.

She wraps her arms around herself, shrugs, It's all I got.

It's not enough.

What do you want from me? I can't—

I thought you were dead. After Jonah's accident. Nobody had any idea. I couldn't believe you would just leave. Not a word. And never call.

Rob's guts churn. Accident? she whispers. So what are you doing?

For sure not waiting around till my number comes up. If it does and I have to go...I wanted to see you before—

As in the draft? Holy shit. Don't you get out because of college?

I dropped out. Lost my scholarship.

Jesus. What happened?

I couldn't do it. After a year and a half I saw my life laid out in front of me and it made me want to barf— play ball for somebody I could care less about, proba- bly fuck up my knees, hang around with mostly stupid jocks, knock up some cheerleader during mediocre sex, not make the pros, work at a used car lot, or worse, with my father.

I can see how that would be pretty bleak. Especially the mediocre sex.

Ha! Right? You remember Jack Porter? A couple years ahead of us.

Is he the one who had the metal plate in his head?

No—

Oh I know! He's the one who fell off the tilt-a-whirl and wore that brace that squeaked.

Don't. Robin. It's not funny—

No no! He's the one who—

Quit it! Jack went to Nam right out of high school. Enlisted, the stupid fuck. Came back a one-armed junkie.

That's got to make it hard to shoot up.

Danny can't help himself. He starts laughing. She starts laughing. They laugh until tears stream down their faces.

And Ronny Fitz? Danny says, wiping his eyes. Remember him? They couldn't even find enough pieces of him to send home.

Jesus, she says again. I'm sorry. I am. What are you gonna do?

He pulls a battered book out of his jacket pocket. My Bible, he holds up Mark Satin's *Manual for Draft-Age Immigrants to Canada.*

Really? How do you even know anything about it?

From the American Friends Service Organization.

Won't they put you in jail?

Not in Canada. Not a crime there.

But if you came back.

He shrugs, fills his cup. I might get lucky. Got a really

high number. Actually the last one to be called. But if it does, I'm gone. But fuck that. So art star, what the hell? Mr. Ackroyd?

You recognized him?

Looked just like him. You want a real laugh? Guess where I got all my moves.

Nah!

You think from Debbie? It was Mrs. Ackroyd and her tight capris.

Woah. No!

She came on to me when I was mowing her lawn. I was maybe fifteen.

Rob thinks, Jesus. The Ackroyds. Peyton Place had nothing on us.

I couldn't get any information. Coach wouldn't tell me anything.

He didn't know anything, she murmurs.

It was just dumb luck I saw that ad. My brothers are all rah rah America. My old man is a die-hard Nixonite. I'm a traitor, worse, a coward, if I don't go kill for peace. We had this huge fight, came close to pounding on each other. I couldn't stay there any more. And nobody knows me like you. I needed to see you. You're the only one I wanted to see before, if, I have to go.

I never knew I was that important.

I didn't either. Until you were gone. I was such an asshole.

They sit in silence, the rooftop giving up the day's warmth into the late September air.

What happened with you? With Debbie?

Are you kidding? She dumped me when I dropped out. I can barely believe we stayed together so long. You? You with anybody?

Nah. Not now. Not really. Come inside. I made stew. You hungry?

After all that gallery cheese? He hands her the wine bottle at the top of the fire escape, turns to head down backwards.

Rob finishes washing their bowls, wipes her hands on her overalls. I should go back to the gallery. Mick will probably—

Danny eyes the bed in the corner of the room. That looks pretty comfy. And way way bigger than the dug-out.

We had fun up there, didn't we, she says, choking up a little.

No! Did I make you cry again?

I don't know what's happening to me. It's like every single little thing lands on my head like a ton of bricks.

I thought artists were hard-assed narcissists.

You get that from Rolling Stone?

I missed you, Puck. All of you. Everything.

Even the concrete burns you got on your knees?

He smiles. Even that.

Come here. Look, I want to show you. She takes him

to her work bench, the prototype for *Catch* hanging on the wall beside it.

Oh man, he whispers, running his fingers over the smooth wood, These are?

She nods.

You really got it. You remembered my hands.

Rob wakes to find herself lying on her side, curled into a ball, Danny's arms and legs surround her like a cocoon. She rests there, unwilling to disturb a sense of safety she has never felt.

He comes to, laughs, This is so great. Look! I can roll over twice before falling out. It's like owing a whole island. He begins massaging her shoulders, her biceps. You are so damned strong, he says. I forgot, how good you feel, so different, how good you are—

Had a good teacher.

Nah. It wasn't me. You're a natural.

Why does everybody say that?

Everybody? You got an everybody?

Ha ha. Tell me.

What do I know? I look like Hugh Hefner? It's just somehow you're always right—like catching a long ball—right place, right time. You know what I want before I do. And you get turned on so easily. It can take some girls so long—

This meditation guy I know says I'm introspective, maybe empathetic.

As in someone who is nice to people? You?

She punches him in the arm. That's sympathetic.

Mostly you sure smell a whole lot better without chest protector sweat.

She wants to tell him, tell him everything, but can't find a way to even begin. He saw us up there once, she blurts out, at the ballfield. Teddy Ackroyd. That's why I, that and the bike.

Danny shakes his head.

She jumps out of bed, pulls on her clothes, says, Bet you never had a Yonah Schimmel knish. Here, she grabs her sketchbook off a shelf, sets it on the bed beside him. This is better, I think. Read this. If you want you can read this. If you want. She grabs Benny's leash, the dog leaps off the bed. We'll be back in about an hour.

The loft is empty when she returns, the door un-locked. His denim jacket is on the chairback but he is not there, not on the roof. Her diary is lying on the kitchen table. She tears down the stairs thinking, he wouldn't just leave, after reading that would he just leave and not say anything. Why not? I left without saying anything. She blasts the front door open and there he is, climbing out of a beat-up Dodge Dart.

I left your door open! he yells. Sorry! Didn't think it would take so long. Man, there are a lot of one-way streets around here. He reaches to hold her, Jesus Puck. We lived five houses away. I was with him nearly every day for years! How did I never know, nobody knew, you never said. I can't—

She backs away. Not now, not now. Did you bring a—

He reaches in the back seat, holds up a football with one hand.

Oh thank god, she whispers, yells, Wait here. She runs upstairs, gives a confused Benny a bowl of food, grabs the bag with the knishes, locks the door, nearly trips on the stairs going down, joins him on the sidewalk.

Let's walk. Walk with me.

He tucks the ball under one arm, matches her stride.

Except for a wino sleeping it off on a bench, they are alone in Sara Roosevelt Park. Rob jukes right, yells Slant Left and takes off on the beat-up grass. The ball is right on the money. She feels the sting, hears the slap, holds it tight before tossing it back in a perfect spiral. They play in silence, the ball passing between them easily, naturally.

He wasn't like that with me, Danny yells from across the field. He was good to me. No other adult treated me like he did, like my opinion mattered, that what I said mattered, was worth listening to. I liked him, I think I maybe loved him. How could he be that way? To you? To Jonah?

It sure didn't seem hard.

He was just so different. With us, the team.

Yeah? How?

He was a hard ass. But he was fair. You wanted him to like you, respect you. He wasn't mean, like you wrote, not ugly. So fucking nasty. He was even funny. He was sometimes, I don't know, a lot like you.

She fires the ball at his head. I am NOTHING like—

He bats the ball to the side. I can't believe I didn't know. Why didn't you say--

I couldn't.

Why not?

I knew you wouldn't have picked me.

He drops his arms, stares at her. She reaches down, gets the ball. He sits on one of the splintered benches, she paces in front, tosses the ball up and down.

I am just...I don't know what I am, he babbles. You have to go back and tell. Tell everybody.

What the hell for? You think they'd believe me?

So he's just going to get away with—

There's no law against being an asshole to your kids.

Somebody should have seen, somehow.

It doesn't matter anymore.

Hell with everybody else, but you need to tell him —

Drop it, Danny.

Why didn't you make his head? For the show?

Yeah. I tried, really wanted to. But it wouldn't come to me. Wouldn't come into my hands. What did he say, about Jonah?

That he fell down the basement stairs.

Motherfucker.

Danny turns to face Rob head on. Why didn't I know, see any of it? I really liked that kid. We talked about everything! I should have—

It was my fault, what he did.

Nah!

He knew I was going to leave, knew I didn't love him enough, enough to stay.

Robin, he talked about it. To me. About suicide. How to do it. More than one time.

And you never said?

It was Jonah! I thought he was doing his thing. You know how he talked about stuff, was interested in everything—medieval tortures, how many suckers on a giant squid, what happens to your brain on Mars. He talked about anything and everything.

Not about that. Not to me! It was. I feel...

She cradles the ball, sits on the bench next to him, lays her head back, stares at the sky.

I should have been nicer. Better. I was mean to him. Sometimes. I didn't love him enough, not nearly enough.

She starts to cry. He reaches to put his arm around her shoulders. She shrugs it off.

And he didn't either, she says as she cries.

Either what?

She cries harder, doesn't try to stop, lets the ball slip to the ground. He didn't love me enough either. He left me alone. It's stupid. I get so mad. How can I get mad at him?

He strokes her arm, recites quietly, Forty thousand sisters could not, with all their quantity of love, make up your sum.

Yeah right. Fuck Hamlet. She wipes her nose with her shirt sleeve, sets her hands hard on the bench seat, pushes herself up.

Oh crap, he says. I think you squished the knish.

She gasps. A joke? she says, Now?

What else have we got?

Rob nods, picks up the ball, Right you are. Only you.

Grabbing mustard and horseradish out of the fridge Rob calls to Danny, Come on, I warmed them up.

Danny comes back from the studio, sits at the table, points to Rob's sketchbook. So I was smart for a jock, huh?

Oh crap. You know what I meant, didn't you? I didn't mean anything—

Nah. It's OK. I know what you meant. It's true. Nobody ever expected me to be good at anything other than throwing a ball, taking a hit. You were the only one I ever did anything different with. You and Jonah. I love tossing the ball around with you Puck, but I'll never play organized ball. Not again.

So what do you want to do?

If I don't have to move to Canada? No clue. It's a whole new universe. And you, you're good with what

you are doing? I see you've got no TV, not even a radio?
What do you do all day?

I make stuff. Take walks. Cook. Seymour gives me
books to read. Sometimes I go to museums. Until Benny
I mostly drank myself to sleep.

What about your stomach? That ulcer thing?

You remember that?

You don't have to have a real job?

What the fuck? Being an artist is a real job.

Yeah, I know. But really, is that enough? You make
enough money?

I've had a couple of part-time jobs but mostly I do OK
from sculpture. Mick sells a lot of it, at least enough of
it. He helped me in the beginning, with money, but I pay
my way now. The sublet rent isn't that much and—

You don't have to do that, in the park—

No! I told you, I sell art!

Sorry. I'm just worried.

Yeah, right.

What is that thing about Anger Management?

Jeez, you don't miss a trick.

It's on the cover of the sketchbook. You cut out letters, made it look like a ransom note.

Oh yeah, she laughs. It was nothing. I got mad at this
woman who cheated me. She pressed charges—

Got mad how?

Threw a brick at her van. No big deal. Doing Anger
Management meant I didn't have to go to jail.

Like that Monopoly card.

Pretty much.

Did you get anything else out of it?

She points to the singing bowl on the bedside table. Actually I did. Have you ever meditated?

Like sit still and breathe? You'll hate it, but Coach had us do that sometimes. With these mind pictures. See yourself winning, see yourself catching the—

I get it.

So what's with the bowl?

Finish eating. I'll show you.

Does knish in English mean lead balloon?

Don't say that too loud around here.

They sit on the bed cross-legged, knees touching. Benny lays next to them, his head on Rob's thigh. Rob sets the bowl on her palm, holds it between them.

Danny points to the dog, He likes it?

Loves it.

So what should I do?

Relax, breathe and listen. Sometimes I see, hear stuff. In my head.

Like?

She shakes her head. Never mind.

They close their eyes, breathe together for a few minutes, easily fall into rhythm. Rob taps the bowl, sends the mallet around the rim slowly. The tones float in the air. Benny grunts, Danny sighs. For once Rob stays completely present, open, not looking for, hoping for her mother's voice, not trying to block out Coach. Her strokes on the bowl's edge become harder, faster. The tones spin wildly, like an aural kaleidoscope. Danny gasps. Rob waits for it, for her mother's voice, sure it will come now. Danny reaches, pokes her on the knee, startles her. She drops the mallet, notices that Benny has moved to the foot of the bed, watches them carefully. The tones fade slowly.

You OK?

Danny nods, stretches out onto his back, pulls Rob next to him. Benny stirs, lays on Rob's other side, his snout on her chest.

Staring at the ceiling Danny speaks in a quiet voice. It all came back. That first time. With Mrs. Ackroyd. I never even knew I remembered. I forgot what it felt like. I was fourteen, no just turned fifteen, been fumbling around with Debbie for fucking ever. I was mowing the lawn, had been mowing the Ackroyd's lawn for a few years. It was hot. She invited me in, gave me a Coke, told me to sit at the kitchen table. She brought a cold cloth, started wiping my forehead, my neck. Then she dropped the cloth, started rubbing my neck and chest with her hands, her cheek next to mine. She smelled like my mother, that Prell shampoo. I froze, just sat there. Here it was, every boy's wet dream, and I was terrified.

Totally terrified. She took my hand, led me to a bedroom. Not the master, just a small bedroom that had a twin bed with a blue blanket. I just stood there. I was totally turned on but confused, scared, barely breathing. She took off her clothes, all of them, everything. Then pulled off my t-shirt, laid her chest against my chest and I came. In my shorts. She laughed. Said something like, We'll have to work on that. But you're young. Let's lie down. And she fucked me, showed me how to fuck her. It was like I was watching a movie and being in a movie. I was there, but wasn't there. Then she looked at the alarm clock on the bedside table, sighed, pushed me off her, said Get dressed. In the kitchen she gave me a ten dollar bill. I never got more than six for mowing the lawn. It went on, for about a year, every couple of weeks. She made up some job, mow the lawn, clean the garage, put stuff in the attic. And there was always money afterward. Ten bucks every time.

Rob turns to see that he is softly crying.

I should be grateful, right? Happy? I never thought about it much, never felt much about it. Never told anyone.

You didn't want to brag? To your friends. I mean really. You wouldn't have had to say who—

I didn't want anybody to know, it was like I was embarrassed or something.

You didn't start it.

No, but I kept going back.

I kept going back with Teddy.

Yeah but you were scared he'd tell Coach.

She shrugs, Yeah, but I also wanted the bike.

Don't rip yourself up about the damned bike, Puck. You never got it anyway.

She laughs. True. Seems like a million years ago.

I barely thought about her, never knew what to feel about it. There was something about what you did with that bowl, those tones, that made it come clear. I know what I feel. Ripped off. Not even mad, just ripped off. I don't know how else to say it.

Rob wipes his tears with the bed sheet. Crap, she says, when you think about it, with babysitting, blow jobs and this, we made a fortune off the Ackroyds.

Ha! He sits up abruptly, pushes her hand away. What a fucking day! Got any more secrets?

I'm so ready to be done with secrets.

Hey. Never say never.

You disappeared again, Mick says as they approach his table at Fanelli's the next morning. What is it with you and openings, kiddo?

Yeah. I couldn't. It was too intense. Hey, this is my friend.

Danny sticks out his hand, says, Dan Cassidy.

Mick shakes his hand, looks at Rob, says, Grace? Is she going to—

No. She is definitely not going to commission one.

Mick sets his fork down. All over, that? You good?

She thinks I'm Conan the Barbarian's mother or something. Yeah, that's over. And yeah, it's alright. I'm good.

The waiter brings one cup of coffee, one plate of toast and scrambled eggs.

I didn't know we'd have company, Mick points at Danny.

I'm good, he says, already ate.

Early riser, you? Well Grace may not want a sculpture but twenty-seven other people do, actually twenty-two. That woman really does want five. It's all set up, kiddo. Once they give us the picture and the payment, we have sixty days to deliver. I already have seven photos for you to get started on.

My cut?

Four hundred a head.

Danny whistles, That's almost eleven grand.

Good with numbers, are you Dan?

Danny rests his hands on the table, slaps the salt shaker from side to side.

You saw Stevenson's review?

She shakes her head.

You didn't?

I've, we've been busy.

Mick lays the paper on the table, So. Where'd you find Dan?

Danny sits back in his chair, We've known each other forever —

Ah. Rob has been very secretive about her past.

Danny was in my high school. My friend. He was a football player.

Any good?

Hell yes—

Danny waves her off. Yeah, I was pretty good, actually damn good, but so was she. Better than most of the team.

Rob laughs, I wish—

He turns to her, Yeah, "kiddo." You had it all, the skills, the instincts, the drive. All you didn't have was the size.

And a cock, she mutters

So an art star and an all-star? Mick asks.

Why not? Rob says. Why the hell does it always have to be one or the other? I am so sick of being either or. I want to be and. But fuck it. None of that's important, not any more.

Dan here looks pretty important to you, no?

Rob scowls at Mick, takes up the paper, scans the review. She reads, Once again Morgan walks a fine line between entertainment and art —What the hell? Entertainment?

Mick dismisses her with a wave. If you had stayed around to talk to him—

Rob gripes, Yeah—

Just keep reading.

Her new work speaks to the needs of people, especially women, to find suitable outlets for their anger, their fears. Although she may not have intended it, the deliberate destruction of her finely-wrought clay sculptures presents us with a dilemma. Are we to believe that we are better off confronting what has hurt us, facing our fear, by destroying it? Or, in its violent destruction, are we simply becoming what injured us, becoming what we fear.

Whoa, Danny says. Good question.

That's not it at all! Rob slams the paper down on the table. It's about taking control—

Doesn't matter, Mick says, sipping the last of his coffee. Doesn't matter even a little. People are talking. Melanie already got you an interview with *Avalanche*, she's making a pitch to *Real Life*. He holds up his coffee cup in a toast, To Rob Morgan, the next New Young Thing.

Danny picks up Rob's fork, clinks Mick's coffee cup, turns to Rob. I guess I am a little hungry, he says and pats her hand. OK?

Sure, she says, sliding the plate over to him, leave me a piece of toast.

When Danny heads for the rest room Mick says, Don't disappear again.

I'll be around.

How long is he here for?

I don't know. Why?

What is he to you?

What's it to you?

Just making sure you're ok.

I'm ok. I'm fine. He's a really old friend.

Well, don't forget your new ones.

Mick, you can't be. Jealous?

Of a kid? Just making sure you're around to do the heads.

the girl and her mother stare at the sleeping toddler. her mother tucks his thin, baby curls behind his ears. he is so beautiful, isn't he? you have to be there for him Puck, he is special. aren't I special too? of course sweetheart, but he is different, not as strong as you. how do you know? I can see, see it in his eyes. no, I mean how do you know I am strong. she hugs the girl close, says, how could you be anything else. he will need your help, you have to be there for him.

Rob wakes, her pillow soaked. She slips out from under Danny's arm, throws on jeans and a T shirt, climbs to the roof. In the sky is the full Hunter's Moon. The city is unusually quiet, the October air chilled. She hears him climbing the fire escape. As he crests the edge of the roof, the moonlight illuminates his hair, the steel struts cast stark thin shadows across his bare chest.

Damn, she thinks, he is so beautiful. What do all these beautiful people see in me. Hey, she calls, You should play Oberon. To my Puck.

I'll come back in mid-summer. As he sits at the table he asks, Bad dream?

I was supposed to protect him.

He was your brother, not your child. You were just a kid.

But she told me to—

It wasn't fair.

She loved him more. I was jealous, believe that? Of my brother.

What was she like?

Like Ariel. With a little Ophelia thrown in maybe.

Magic and crazy?

I guess. I was only ten when she died. I don't know what I'm remembering. I want so much to remember her. Come back inside. I want to show you.

She drags the duffel out of the closet, digs out the portfolio, lays out the portraits, says, Jonah did those from some photos he found.

God, he looked just like her.

Yeah. And I sure didn't. She opens the sketchbook, Here, this is what I wanted you to see.

Danny gasps, is silent as he pages through the vividly colored drawings of Jonah murdering Coach.

It's was all he had, the only way he could get back at him. Did he ever say anything to you?

Not about any of it, he points to the notebook, never about this. What a fucking waste. He was really good.

Way better than me.

Not better. Different. Who would have thought you'd be the next, he makes air quotes, New Young Thing?

Not me, that's for fucking sure.

She would be proud. I bet she would be proud.

Rob stands, takes a pose, sings quietly,

Fear no more the heat of the sun nor the furious winters' rages.

Though your worldly task is done, home art gone and taken your wages.

Golden lads and girls all must, As chimney sweepers, come to dust.

He shakes his head.

From *Cymbeline*, one of those confusing nobody-is-who-you-think-they-are plays. She used to sing it to us.

Seems pretty intense to sing to kids.

Guess so. Never thought of that. She takes one of his arms, drapes it around her shoulder, squeezes his hand. Hell, I don't know if I ever was a kid.

They sit in the bath, knees up, facing each other.

I could get used to this, Danny says. He points to Rob's sketchbook on the kitchen table, mimics Mick's voice, A very eventful couple of years you've had Rob Morgan, no?

He's alright. He just acts like a jerk sometimes.

Do you and he—

She shrugs. Yeah. Sometimes.

Isn't he a little old?

Like Mrs. Ackroyd wasn't?

That was just fucking. You don't owe him anything.

I do. Sort of.

You don't have to pay that way. Looks like you're making him a bundle of cash.

It's not paying! He stood up for me when I had nothing. Nobody. I'd maybe be dead if not for Mick.

Seems like he's using you.

If anybody is using anybody it's me using him! Walk around here, you won't see a lot of galleries showing women, much less total unknowns. Mick is willing to take a chance—

You could have come home—

That was never my home!

So you love him?

No! Some. Maybe. I don't even know what that means.

He isn't gonna love you, not like that.

You think I don't know!

Crap, I made you cry again. Why are you so sad?

Not sad. Not only. Happy too.

Yeah?

Happy because you are here, sad because you will most likely leave. Everybody leaves. And I had no idea how much I've missed just talking, how tired I am of watching what I say, remembering who I told what to, holding back. I am worried all the damn time.

The art star? What do you have to worry about?

Getting found out! I've been lying my ass off, to everybody. Telling the world that Jonah's portfolio is my work. I never told Mick about Deborah, or the park. I lied to Grace about Mick, pretended that I hate football. I love football. I should hate it but I don't. And mostly lying my whole fucking life about Coach. I never even cried for Jonah until you came. I'm always worried, scared. Sometimes it feels like I never left New Jersey.

Danny turns so that his back is resting on Rob's chest. She feels the full weight of him, wraps her arms around his neck.

How about you come with me.

To Canada?

To wherever.

Now you ask that?

I was such a jerk. Why did I pick Debbie Myers.

Because she could do the splits.

You could do the splits.

Yeah, but she was pretty.

You weren't—

Don't I know it.

He pinches her knee. I was gonna say that you are better than pretty, there's a lot of pretty out there, there's only one you.

Thank god for that, she murmurs. Besides, you and me on a date? Coach would have found some way to fuck it up. I never could chance it, never knew what he might do. Never went out with anybody, even once. I was always cleaning that stupid fucking house. And you and me? We were destined to NOT be together. Hell, how could Debbie the head cheerleader and Danny the quarterback not have ended up together. No way you could have gotten out of that.

He declaims, Men at some time are masters of their fate. The fault, dear Robin, is not in our stars, but in ourselves.

Yeah right.

Don't you think so?

I feel like I've been pushed around by the stars my whole life. What do I know?

He lays his head against her shoulder, sloshing a little water over the lip of the tub.

Your hair, she says as she puts it in a loose braid, I love it. Why did you grow it?

Mostly to piss off my father.

It's so beautiful. I miss having long hair.

I like you like this, but couldn't you just grow it out?

I sort of made friends with this barber. Like to see him once in a while.

Why did you cut it in the first place?

This guy grabbed my braid, tried to hurt me.

When you were doing that, in the park?

You can say it.

Did he? Hurt you?

Nah. I cut his arm a little, got away.

Good. So you never went to school? To finish?

What, and do homework between blow jobs on a park bench?

Was it gross?

Yeah it was gross. It definitely wasn't sexy. Sorry but I don't want to do that again, to anyone. Ever. Jeez it seems like a lifetime ago. Do you see her? Remember her? When you fuck?

Mrs. Ackroyd? Nah. It WAS a lifetime ago. She was a blip.

So why did it make you cry to remember her?

More like I was remembering me. Losing some piece of me.

I was stuck, totally stuck, when I got here. Had no idea what to do, where to go. The blow job thing was only really bad if I thought about it. Usually I could block it out while it was happening.

That counting in your head thing?

She nods, Forgot I told you about that, then laughs, Sometimes I spent the whole time wondering why it was called a blow job when it should have been called a suck job.

He grabs her hands, squeezes them. Only you, he says. And what about that woman you lived with.

Deborah. Yeah.

What's it like? Sex with a woman.

You don't know?

Really, come on. Is it different?

Sure. Some. Not really. You connect or you don't, doesn't matter who it is. It's all body parts. Sometimes it's just getting off. Sometimes it's like a different way of talking. Deborah was usually so stoned she just fell asleep.

And that other woman, from the gallery? The one you looked at before you smashed Ackroyd? Is that the Grace Mick talked about?

Jeez. You really don't miss a trick.

So? What's that about? Do you love her?

Nah. I don't know. I think I was just playing the game. Feeling good.

You think she loved you?

She said so. But it seemed more like she wanted to collect me.

I mean it. Why don't you come with me? I would play catch with you. Every day.

That the sexiest thing anyone has ever said.

I don't know, Puck. I don't know what's going on. I know I don't want to collect you. Or use you. But I do know I want to be around you.

Rob pushes him off her chest, steps out of the tub, wraps up in a towel and sits at the table. Benny pads over, stands next to her, nuzzles her leg. She scratches between his ears. So what's with all this stuff about love? I thought you said it was just a game, just another way to play.

Danny stands, lets the water slide off his body. He grabs a towel, sits next to her, Benny between them. Nah, he says. Sex is a game. Sex isn't love.

What is?

I was hoping you'd tell me. Except for Coach, you're the only person I ever had any kind of real conversation with.

You can't be serious.

All I know is that love has to be more than just making somebody feel good.

So maybe why don't you just stay here for a while? With me? Until you're called up?

Would it just be me?

She laughs. As in—Jesus, Danny—like you want to go steady?

He shrugs.

Yeah. Ok. Why not.

Don't do me any favors.

No, I'm good. I'm into it. I want you here. Really. I just have to make sure I have time to work.

How about I get in your way when you want me to get in your way.

She drops her towel, straddles him. That would be a couple times a day easy.

And one more thing. Now that you are Rob no more Danny. I want to be Dan.

Dan. Yeah, I get it. It will be a stretch, but I'll try. I'll try to get used to that.

Dan sets the back issue of *ArtNews* aside, watches Rob from the corner of her studio. Benny snores softly at his feet. She kneads a ball of clay, slaps it onto the metal armature, steps back, studies the drawings she has made from the client's photo.

Later for you, she murmurs, startles when she notices Dan.

You want me to leave?

No, don't. I'm done for now.

I really like watching you. You look so much the same.

She lights a cigarette. Yeah?

When you're working. Same as when you're playing ball.

What? The focus?

Focus for sure but more like you're in a battle, like you're fighting with something.

the broken crayon stains the girl's fingers. her mother pulls the paper from her, smooths it out. you have to be more gentle, Robin. watch Jonah. don't be so rough. you look like your father when you do that.

Fighting?

Not bad fighting, not like you're pissed off or anything. More like you're pulling something out of yourself. And it isn't easy.

She scoffs, then smiles. You checked at the gallery? No mail?

He shakes his head. My mother promises to forward it.

It's driving me crazy, not knowing if you'll have to go.

Being born on September 24th, who knew it would ever matter.

Hey it's been three months.

Since?

My opening.

An anniversary! We have to celebrate. Jones Beach? Too cold. How about Bear Mountain? Benny really liked it there.

I should finish—

How many heads have you done?

Twenty-eight.

You just gonna keep going?

It is sort of getting old.

So tell him you want to stop.

Yeah, maybe I will. Bear Mountain. Great idea. You want to ask Seymour?

I would, but he's gone for a few days.

I'm glad you guys are friends.

He's a trip. Sort of like Jonah, he knows something about everything. Those tin boxes of his blow my mind. I'll get the car. It's over on West Broadway. I think. The parking rules around here drive me crazy.

Dan brings the Dodge around, sees Rob in front of

their building being air kissed goodbye by a woman who is dressed so stylishly she has no need to work at being stylish. He wonders if she is Grace.

Rob lets go of Benny's lead and the dog jumps into the back seat. As she gets in the car she says, Wow, you'll never believe it. The queen of the Soho art scene wants me.

Wants how?

Wants me, to represent me, sell my work.

Ah, that kind of want, he murmurs as he gets behind the wheel. That's good! So what did you tell her?

I told her no. What else am I gonna tell her.

Without even thinking about it? What did she offer?

A contract for five years.

Do you even have a contract with Mick?

No but.

Do you even know how much he's making from your work?

Sure. I think. There's the sales price and my cut. He gets the rest.

And that's how much?

Give it a rest, Danny! Dan. I'm not leaving Mick. Fuck. I didn't even know I could be an artist before him.

I just—

You're just what? Worried about us fucking? We're not together anymore, not that way. But he's in my life, always will be. Get over it. And for Christ's sake I'm not this thing you two pass back and forth.

I know, I know.

What then, what the fuck?

Forget it, he says and pulls into traffic, I'm just on edge too, hate wondering even more than you do. I'm just as bad as you at waiting.

Seymour and Dan slide the 4x8 foot pane of plate glass slowly out of the bed of the pickup, walk it carefully across the sidewalk. Mick holds open the gallery door. They set it against the wall on blocks of wood, go back to the truck for tools and caulk guns. The front window, cracked for years, needs to be replaced before Mick can get his deposit back.

Rob is in the back room wrapping and crating the last head, a small balding man wearing over-sized eyeglasses. Number fifty. She has told Mick not to accept any more commissions. Although he isn't thrilled, he can't complain. Because of the success of Rob's show and the attendant publicity, he will be moving to a much larger space, a few blocks south, right between two of the heavy hitters. Every day artists arrive in his office, lugging their huge portfolios full of artwork and nervous anticipation, yearning for representation.

Seymour opens a can of putty with a car key while Dan uses a screwdriver and hammer to chisel the old caulk from around the window frame.

So Dan, Mick says, what do you know about glass installation?

The kid is good with pretty much anything, Seymour says. He's got a gift.

It's my old man's business, Dan answers. Glass and mirrors. I helped in the summers.

Not taking over the family business?

Dan scoffs. No way in hell. I was supposed to be the football star, rescue them all from the middle class.

Didn't quite work out, yes?

Dan starts to tell him to shove it, takes a breath. He is working at it, trying to like Mick. Instead he asks, How about your father?

In business? Not. I am the blackest of black sheep. Not only am I not in academia, I am in, he makes air quotes, "commerce." Even though it's art related, it's still de classe. He's a Professor of French literature. Medieval French literature that no one except his students have read in millennia.

Dan laughs, Seymour probably has.

The only one I remember, Seymour says, is *Chanson de la croisade albigeoise*. First part written by William of Tudlea. Nobody is sure who wrote the second part.

What did I tell you.

You never cease to amaze, Mick says. What about your father, Seymour? What was he?

A drunk.

Dan and Mick look at each other.

But a nice drunk, Seymour continues. And rich as shit.

How rich is that, Dan asks.

Like I grew up at 1001 Fifth Avenue rich.

Mick whistles. That building across from the Met?

Where do you think I learned what I know? Olga dropped me off after school and told me to get lost until dinner time.

Your mother was Russian?

How's that?

Named Olga?

That's a hoot! Olga was my au pair.

Mick and Dan say, You had an au pair?

And a cook.

Tell me she wasn't black, Danny says.

The cook, yeah, Cornelia. The au pair was Romanian. Told me her family worked at Bran Castle for centuries.

The Dracula Castle?

Seymour nods, smiles. She used to try to scare me, say she was a vampire. But she went home at night. I had the place all to myself. He calls to the back room, How about your old man, Rob?

Dan says quickly, He's a Phys Ed teacher. And a football coach. He was my coach.

Rob has been listening. She wipes her hands down the sides of her jeans, sits silent beside the crate she has just finished packing.

Dan and Seymour jimmy the cracked pieces of glass out of the window.

Look at that the thickness of that slab, Seymour says. So clean, clear. Such great workmanship.

Be careful, Mick says. It looks razor sharp.

Dan nods, sets the pieces carefully against the far

wall. I'll put them in the truck later. How about your mother, Mick, he asks, working to keep the conversation away from Rob.

The long-suffering wife of a pompous but handsome professor, Mick says. She put up with his affairs for nearly twenty years, then to everyone's surprise demanded a divorce. She's happy now. Actually into Women's Lib. I see her once a month or so, an uptown dinner date.

I never had much to do with my mother, Dan says. It was just like, just, she was there. We never talked much beyond, pick up your dirty socks, what do you want for breakfast. My biggest mental image of her is making sandwiches on the kitchen counter. I have four brothers, five of us big boys in one house. We were always starving. For lunches she must have laid out an entire loaf of bread every day—mayonnaise, mustard, bologna or spiced ham. When she got fancy there was some lettuce. Or a slice of tomato. We each got two and a peanut butter and jelly for dessert. She made like fifteen sandwiches. Every day. He laughs, She was this sandwich making machine.

Mine was always traveling, Seymour says, didn't see her much, much less talk to her. A world traveler. Came home at Christmas, sometimes. She died, somewhere in Egypt, when I was about fifteen.

That's kind of sad, Dan says.

Not really. No reason to miss something you never had.

What about Olga? Did you think of her like a mother?

Seymour laughs. Her sole piece of wisdom was—he holds his hands, palm up at chest level and says in a strong Slavic accent, You can wish in this hand and shit in that one and see which one fills up faster. I think she hated us, hated that we were rich. But the old man left her a bundle and she moved to Florida. He lays down his tools, says, Let's get this baby in the frame.

Mick yells, Rob! We need you. Aren't you finished with that crate?

Dan steps into the back room, sees Rob sitting on the floor, leaning on the side of the desk.

She looks up. I'm OK, she says. Leave me. I'll be right there.

Sure?

I'm said I'm OK!

Thanks for joining us, yes? Mick snipes when Rob comes into the gallery.

Dan leans toward Mick, says in a quiet voice, It's time you left her alone, yes?

Rob stands between them. Will you both just fucking quit it!

How about we work on one thing at a time, Seymour says, handing Dan two industrial-sized suction cups.

Dan clamps the cups, grabs the far side of the glass, lifts his end. Rob and Mick step forward, ready to brace it once it is set in place. It sticks a bit on one end. They take it down, chisel out more of the frame, try it again. Perfect fit. Dan spreads beads of caulk across the top and bottom edges, Seymour does the sides.

Here's the trick, Seymour says as he wets a small section of thin cloth, wraps it around his index finger and runs it in a slow, single stroke over the caulk beads—a perfect line to ensure a strong seal. It takes practice, he says quietly, but you gotta smooth it over.

You made it, Mick, Rob tells him. This place is really beautiful. It's gotta be at least five times bigger than the old space.

Yeah! Mick is unusually enthusiastic. And it's got a ton of storage so I can finally carry back stock. Still needs a lot of work, but it's going to be amazing. He points to an alcove in the east wall. Over there, that's where the counter will go. I'll be printing catalogues of the shows. Already hired Melanie, an actual gallery assistant.

She scoffs, About time.

You're going to get offers, kiddo. Other galleries.

Already have.

The fuckers. And?

You have to ask?

You're sure? Make sure you're sure. You'd get a real bump for your career—

Forget it, Mick. You're stuck with me.

He throws an arm around her shoulders, hugs her close. You helped me get here, Rob, you know that right? Hell, you did more than help. If it wasn't for you, I might not be here.

She pokes him in the chest, pushes him away. And
hell, if it wasn't for you, I would definitely not be here.
Kiddo.

It's working for you? You and Dan?

It's good, yeah.

A football player, huh.

Come on already! He's way more than—

Just kidding. I can see that. I'm happy for you. Really.

Then be nice to him why don't you.

I will, I will. I am. So, it's all business, you and me. He
pulls his hand from his jacket pocket, offers it for her to
shake. We're all business, yes?

She takes it, holds on, waits to feel that spark, fears
that she might feel it. But all she feels is his hand in hers.
She tightens her grip. And friends? she says. Business
and friends?

Of course, kiddo, never not friends.

Rob smiles, shakes his hand, lets it go.

He walks her over to the floor-to-ceiling frosted glass
window. So. We'll open in about a year. You'll be first up,
yes?

Jeez. That's a quick turn around. It's harder now. I
sort of have a life, actually do things.

It's got to be you kiddo. And it's got to be good. They'll
be coming for you, after *Restitution*—critics, writers,
other artists.

This is a big space—

You have to be the first.

She walks to the center of the room, opens her arms

and spins slowly in a wide circle. Yeah, ok, she says, thinking, Christ almighty, this place is huge.

Rob yells, Goddamngoddamngoddamn!

The loft door opens. Benny comes bounding through, slides to a halt when he sees Rob ready to chuck a chisel across the studio. Dan hangs up the leash, peers around the corner.

All good?

NO! I'm stuck, so fucking stuck I will never be un-stuck. I've got seven months—

Why don't you just tell him you can't be ready in time, that—

Why don't you just shut the fuck up!

Benny barks, Rob throws up her hands.

I'm sorry! I didn't mean—

He shakes his head. You're right. This is wrong. I need to not be here—

No! I need you. Need you to stay.

I won't go far. Just downstairs. Seymour said I can use part of the second floor. You won't believe it. The whole front of the loft is furnished like something out of that 1940s Bob Hope movie. Bamboo and rattan all over the place. Sofas, tables, even a hammock slung across the room. Did you know this is his building?

Seymour owns this fucking building?

Yeah. It was one of his father's—

You talked about this with him already? About me?

Yeah, some. You're getting—

Getting what! What? What the fuck am I getting?

This!

She glares at him, then plunks down on a stool. Jesus. Danny. Dan. I'm a mess.

A little more than usual, for sure.

I can't shake it. I feel like a phony. Like I'll never get another idea in my entire life. Like all I want to do is get drunk and go to sleep.

How about we take a walk? Or you. Why don't you go by yourself?

Now you don't even want to walk with me?

For Christs sake!

Kidding. Just kidding. Let's walk uptown. Hit the Modern.

After a few turns around the upstairs galleries, Dan and Rob ride the down escalator. She points out the window to the museum's sculpture garden. There's a Henry Moore I really like.

Massive. But somehow still gentle.

Good eye!

Don't sound so surprised. Smart for a jock, aren't I?

Rob steps off the escalator. You remember that. It really hurt? What I wrote?

Some. Not much. A little. Besides it was true. What the hell did I know about anything else? I had such a nothing life. Every damn day, from eight years old on, my life was about nothing but football. I didn't have to think, was told what to do, how to do it, was expected to be good, to prove them all right. Not expected to be good at anything else. It wasn't so bad, not anything like your life, I wasn't afraid like you were. I had some talent, got a lot of strokes for it. But I was a little afraid, all the time. Afraid I'd fail, afraid to disappoint Coach. So I've always wondered what I'd do, if it wasn't for football. I don't know, hanging around with you, with Seymour, watching you both make things, I just wonder, wonder what I missed. So I've been reading up on this art stuff. Between you guys there must be five thousand books and magazines in the building. It makes me think.

About? What are you interested in?

Anything! Everything! Who knows? He waves his arms in a big circle, Actually I'm really interested in this.

This building? The air?

Listen.

She stands still, cocks her head. Yeah?

The sounds, you hear all the sounds? And the silences, how they are a thing, not just what's in between the sounds.

Interesting. What do you—

Never mind. I have no idea what I'm talking about. He points to the Moore piece, You ever going to work with stone?

No clue. I never have any idea what the hell I'm doing. Just go with my gut. Mick took me here, a bunch of times, when we first met. I came back by myself, on free days, just wandered, looked. Learned more doing that than I ever did in any class. Here, come this way. Can't leave without seeing *Guernica*. They just finished cleaning it after some moron spray painted it.

As they turn toward the gallery with the famous painting, Rob spots Grace and another woman coming towards them. Grace looks as good as she always does but the woman with her is stunning. As tall as Dan but slender like a reed. She wears a simple long-sleeved black dress that falls to her ankles just above her scuffed Doc Martens. Her blonde hair shoots out from her head, a Medusa of curls. When she smiles, Grace lights up like a Christmas tree. Rob plucks at the neck of her baggy sweater, hikes up her jeans, ruffles her hair, then yanks Dan's arm, tries to pull him in the opposite direction.

Rob? It is you!

Hey, yeah. Grace. Crap she thinks, but smiles and says, Hi.

How great to see you! Lucy, this is Rob Morgan, the one who made that sculpture in my living room.

Wow, Lucy says, extending her hand for Rob to shake. I love that piece!

Rob looks down at her hand for a second, shakes it. And this, she points, this is Dan.

Dan nods, smiles, says, Nice to finally meet you.

Grace furrows her brow. You know who I am?

Why wouldn't I, Dan says with a smile, Rob and I go way back.

I see, she turns to Rob, You just getting here?

Last stop, Rob says, pointing to *Guernica*.

Let's get a drink. After? It would be great to catch up.

Nah, I—

That would be wonderful, Dan butts in.

Rob gives him the side eye. No, I really—

Lucy nods. Yeah, let's. I'd love to talk to you about that *Disfigure* piece.

Grace beams, Lucy is an artist too! A painter. They'll be closing here soon. How about we meet at that place we went to. The one around the corner on 6th?

Yeah, yeah, Rob mutters. We'll be out in a few.

Dan wanders into the room, stands with crossed arms before the huge mural. As annoyed as she is at him for accepting Grace's invitation, Rob watches intently as his eyes move across the painting.

After several minutes he says quietly, It's like taking a lifetime of blindside hits.

Yes it is, she says. That's exactly what it is.

Nothing changes, does it. Fucking war. Let's get out of here.

As they get their coats and exit the museum, she bumps his shoulder with hers. So we're having a drink with Grace and that amazingly beautiful woman?

He raises his eyebrows, puts his arm around her shoulders, You got good taste. Grace ain't so bad herself. It'll be terrific. Time to have your worlds collide.

The restaurant is quiet, the servers chat with each other as they set up for the dinner rush. Grace and Lucy have taken a booth, four glasses of red wine sit on the table. Grace pours two of the glassfuls into empty coffee cups, sets the now empty wine glasses on a table across from the booth.

I ordered for you, Rob, she says, then stage whispers to Lucy, Still underage maybe, but I taught her to appreciate good wine. You too Dan?

He slides into the booth, sits next to her. He reaches to the empty glasses, refills them with wine from the coffee cups, takes a sniff, then a sip, says, Actually, very much of age.

Grace laughs, Handsome and funny, who would have thought.

Rob takes her seat beside Lucy. Beats Mad Dog all to hell, doesn't it? She turns to her, So you're a painter? Do I know you? Have I seen your work any place?

She's from Chicago, Grace says. That's why you've never heard of her.

Lucy laughs, My last name is Jordan and you haven't heard of me because I'm not famous enough to be heard of anywhere.

Yet, Grace says.

Dan asks, What kind of work do you do?

Big work, Grace says, beautiful work.

Lucy takes Grace's hand across the table, squeezes it, smiles and says, My biggest fan.

Rob takes a gulp of wine, mutters, It's always good to have one of those.

I'm working on a series, Lucy continues, large scale nudes, men and women. Figurative. I know I'm bucking all the trends, but you know, she turns to Rob, you can only do what comes into your hands.

Rob looks, nods. I do know. I know that really well.

Lucy leans across the table toward Dan. You have a very interesting face. And what looks like a beautiful body. Have you ever considered modeling?

He blushes, laughs. No, I haven't. Ever. No.

You should, Lucy says. I'd love to paint you.

Grace sets her nearly empty glass down, says, Hey! I got a notice, from Mick Taylor. About the new gallery?

Rob nods, Yeah, it's a great space.

It said you'll have the first exhibit? Looks like that *Restitution* show put you both in the big leagues?

Lucy lays her hand on Rob's arm, says, Grace told me about that work. Damn, that was really a gutsy move.

Rob pulls her arm away, shrugs.

Grace edges closer to Dan. What did you think?

I think Rob is a really gutsy person. So it stands to reason.

But of the idea? What did you think of the idea of destroying what we hate? Like that?

He turns to face Grace head on, smiles. I've had some things I wanted to destroy like that. Haven't you?

Oh yeah, Lucy says as she reaches across the table for Grace's hand again. I'll bet everybody has. Hey, babe, maybe we should head out?

Grace drains her glass, Yeah. We need to go.

I should hit the rest room, Dan says, we've got a long walk.

Lucy goes to stand, Rob lets her out of the booth. Me too, she says. Grace and I hiked all the way down from Riverside and 84th.

So you're hiking? Rob says to Grace as she sits back down. Watch out, you might even start taking the subway.

Grace smiles, That would be pushing it.

That was quick work. Another artist?

Guess I developed a taste for it. And you? He's quite something? Are you?

I never said I was only—

I know, I know. You're the in-between. You look good together, at home. Someone your age, someone like you.

Like me, huh. So what is like me?

You know how you are. So physical. Powerful.

Is Lucy? Powerful?

Not like you. But powerful, yes. Different. Different kind of power.

I'll say, she mutters as she slides out of the booth,

puts on her coat. Very different.

Rob watches Lucy hand Dan a business card as they wait by the cash registers. He smiles, sticks it in his jacket pocket.

Rob and Dan head south on Sixth Avenue passing noisy electronic stores, Orange Julius stands, single-slice pizzerias, cheap furniture rental centers.

She points to Dan's chest pocket. So Mr. Beautiful Body, you going to do it? Model for Lucy?

Doubt it. Can't see myself standing still for so long. But maybe. She said she pays seven bucks an hour. I could use some cash.

You want cash? I'll give you cash. Stay away from her.

What?

She's just so damned—

Oh for Christ's sake, Rob. She's beautiful? Yeah, so? They both are. Of course I'd like to fuck them both. Maybe even at the same time. Hell. I bet you would too. And it would be just that. Fucking. But neither one of them is you. No way could either of them take a hit. Or catch a long ball.

So you like me for my football skills?

Dan stops, grabs Rob's shoulder, spins her to face him yells, It's a metaphor!

Rob is not listening. In the store window to her right she glimpses a display set up like a living room. Checkered sofa, a glass-topped coffee table, overstuffed arm chair.

the man yells at the top of his lungs. you bought another one? for Christ's sake how many chairs do we need? the woman just shrugs, smiles. get off Jonah, don't you dare get that dirty. it's going back. today. what am I, made of money!

Dan pokes her in the chest, How many times do I have to say it? It's a metaphor! The reason I like you is because of who you are. Where you've been. How you do what you do.

Holy crap, Rob whispers, takes his hand and walks them close to the window. She shades her eyes to block out her reflection, stares at the display.

Are you listening? At all?

Yeah, yeah. And me too. Like you. I know you do. Know I do. But holy holy crap. I got it, Danny. Dan. I got an idea. Maybe THE idea. We have to get home. I need Seymour's truck. Where the hell am I going to find a farm store? I have to learn to use a lathe.

Over the next several months, a few times a week, Rob goes down to have dinner with Benny and Dan on the second floor, trying to have some semblance of their life together. She sometimes stays over, she and Dan have half-hearted sex, more out of habit then desire, she walks Benny in the mornings, then heads back upstairs. She refuses to let anyone into her space since she brought back ten rolls of barbed wire from a feed store in Jersey and had Seymour teach her to use Maria's lathe. Her hands and arms are pocked with small cuts, but she won't say what she's working on. Mick is getting antsy. The gallery renovation is nearly finished, the opening publicity in preparation. Not yet, she tells him, but almost, almost.

Just three weeks before the opening, Rob says to Dan, Leave Benny down here when you all come up. I haven't cleaned up enough yet.

He nods. I'll wait here for the others. You good?

As good as I'm gonna be.

Mick, Seymour and Dan stand just inside the doorway to Rob's loft, stopped in their tracks. She has taken everything—every bench, table, chair, stool, pile of crap, crate, tub, tool chest—that had been in the middle of the studio and pushed it all against one wall. She pulled the newspapers from the window panes, washed off the dried, cracked glue so that what had been a cavern-like space is now flooded with sunlight. An arched doorway made of thickly banded together strands of barbed wire is nailed to a thick slab of wood in the center of the space, forming a threshold. An arrangement of large objects sits beyond it, set up like an apartment with no walls. You pass under the arch into the living room on the left, furnished with a sofa, coffee table and love seat. Set behind that is a dining table and two ladderback chairs. About ten feet to the right of the table is double bed, next to it a rocking chair. Each piece of furniture has uniform legs and struts, beautifully hand-turned maple, white as bone, making the whole arrangement a set. Across the bed frame lies a patchwork quilt, alternating woven squares of shiny and rusty barbed wire. The headboard is a span of twisted barbed wire, the center section formed into an open heart-shape. Except for the curved legs, the rocker is formed entirely of woven and banded barbed wire strands. The wire is strung between the legs of the dining table, creating the tabletop. The chair seats and backs have been treated in the same manner. The cushions of the sofa and love seat are intricately woven barbed wire pillows that are attached to the posts and struts. Arranged in spirals, like a mosaic, barbed wire forms the top of the coffee table. Light pouring in from the newly cleaned windows causes the shiny wire to gleam and flash, the sharp barbs magnified in the shadows, creating elongated strands of blurred but terrifying thorns across the floor.

It's as if the work has cast a spell. No one moves, no one talks. Mick inhales abruptly, starts to speak, falls silent. He moves first, ducks under the arch, wends his way around the furniture, his arms held high and apart from his body. Dan stays on the perimeter, shakes his head, mouths, Only you. Seymour stands next to him, arms crossed, just stares at the shadows on the floor.

Rob can't stand the silence, yells, So? Guys?

Mick asks, Title?

Home, it's called *Home*.

Oh yes, Mick says quietly. Yes. I have no idea how to sell this but I am definitely going to show it.

The spell is broken, Seymour and Dan step under the arch, enter *Home*, examine each piece closely.

Dan looks her in the eye, says quietly, It's so sad—

She shakes her head.

He follows her lead, says, Now I know where you got all those cuts. How in hell did you weave this wire?

She relaxes. Yeah. This stuff is wicked! I nearly blinded myself before I started wearing safety glasses. I made these jigs to wrap it around. Made it easier.

Very clever, Seymour says. And the rusty looking wire that's not really rusty?

Vinegar. Soaked it in vinegar. Took the shine right off. What do you think? I can make more stuff, small stuff. A bowl of fruit on the kitchen table, maybe a book on the coffee table. A couple of pillows on the bed.

Dan says quietly, You maybe don't want to get any more literal.

Seymour nods, It's enough. Close to too much.

Mick looks at them, surprised. They're right. It's good. Just as it is.

Does it need walls? Rob asks, between the rooms?

Easy, Mick says, take it easy. There's plenty of space. An installation like this, we need to figure that out there, in the gallery.

So that's what this is. An installation. I'm glad there is a name for it.

You gotta get out more, kiddo. Now tell me how the hell we get it out of here.

She holds out a cleat and screw. It's put together with these things, not staples like you'd use on a fence. So it comes apart. Easy. Except for the rocker. But that's small enough to fit in the elevator. When you wear gloves it doesn't hurt as much. But I'll need to crate each section of the other pieces separately or they get all tangled.

I can help, Dan says. I really want to help.

Rob exhales, gives him a full body hug. Let's stay downstairs tonight, this place is a pit. We can come back tomorrow, clean everything up, get it ready to go.

Rob rolls on top of Dan, lays her head against his neck, licks off his sweat. Oh my god, I have missed this! Missed you. I can't believe I did it, actually made it in time.

You did. You sure as hell did.

You've been so great, how did you get to be such a good man? And hey, what was that, before, what were you going to say about the work?

He pushes her off gently, sits up against the wall. So you got that idea, that day, walking from the museum? Looking in that furniture store?

Yeah.

And then how? How did it become those pieces. With that wire.

I don't know. I have no idea how it happens. Just felt something, looking at that cheesy furniture. Thought about home. What home means.

It's so damned sad. I hate that it's so sad.

It is what it is.

And so personal. How can you be OK making it public?

Nobody but you knows anything about me.

But everybody is gonna see it, see what you mean. It's so obvious.

I don't care. I'm tired of hiding it.

He starts to cry softly, It's, I don't know, so fucking brave or something.

She sits up next to him. What? What is it really?

I never thought about it before. About home. What mine was like. I was just there, mostly not there. Never wondered what my mother's life was like, never cared about my brothers, automatically hated my old man.

Why? Why automatically?

He was, all I ever was was his ticket out. I was the one to make the big bucks, make it so he could stop working. He hated what he did, always bitching about it. And if we lost a game, or I said I was sick of football, he told me I was a lazy ungrateful bastard. It got so we barely talked to each other. The only real relationship I ever had was with Coach.

Jesus, poor you.

No! You don't get it. You think I'm nice, "a good man." It's because of him. He made me who I am, practically raised me. He was the only person I cared about, wanted to impress. We used to meet in the weight room, a few nights a week, for years, after practice. He talked to me, asked me what I thought, what mattered to me. He was so different from my father.

Did he ever say anything? About me? Or Jonah? My mother?

Never about your mother. Or Jonah. About you, maybe once, once or twice?

Yeah?

He said you were a pretty good cook.

That's it?

I mentioned a few times, how good you were, that you should be on the team. He said the obvious, that you were a girl. When I said maybe the practice squad he said you were not strong enough, didn't have any drive. I wasn't paying attention but I should have noticed. He never saw you. Who you were.

He never looked. And I was different, around him. I was only me when I was away from him.

It doesn't make sense. I can't make it make sense. That he was so shitty to you and Jonah.

It's not rocket science. He loved you.

But why not you? I just want it to make sense, how he could be such a monumental asshole.

Didn't you know that already? You read my diary, what I wrote.

It's different, totally different. Seeing it is different.

Dan sobs, He was so good to me. How could he be that and—

Rob holds him until he calms down, then she starts to laugh, You realize how fucking ironic this is, don't you?

He wipes his face. You made the stuff, I didn't.

Opening day. The pieces are installed, lit, professionally photographed. Melanie has created a fold-out brochure. Stevenson surprisingly agreed to contribute a short statement, "Morgan's work is painful, literally and metaphorically. And heartbreaking. Her beautifully crafted furniture affords a viewer no rest—no place to sit, to lean, to lie. There is no safety, no comfort, in this *Home*."

Dan comes back after taking Benny for his morning walk. Rob sits at the table, head bent, staring at a photograph.

Checked the mail at the gallery, he says. Still nothing from my mother. I know I sent her the new address. What you got there?

She looks up, smiles a fake smile, Hey! Look what I found. She tosses a photograph onto the kitchen table, says, Jeez, yeah, I can see it. Lucy really is a good painter.

You went through my pockets?

For the laundry! I was getting the laundry ready!

Rob, it's not, I just posed.

Yeah, I can see! That's some pose. And life size! It's like I'm looking at you right now! But you'd have to take all your clothes off, huh?

Really, I just wanted to make a few bucks.

Was it like with Mrs. Ackroyd? Oh no, I bet not. With Lucy all you had to do was stand still. Right?

Jesus Christ, Robin!

She looks up at him, down at the photograph, So you just stood there, posed buck naked for the incredibly gifted beautiful painter girlfriend of my beautiful ex-girlfriend—

You said you didn't even like Grace!

And you took Benny? That's my dog, isn't it? Right there the picture! When?

Over the summer. While you were working. Only a few times. It was just a way to make a little money. It was nothing—

If it was nothing why didn't you fucking say something?

You were, in that head space. Mick said not to say anything—

How the fuck does Mick know?

Grace took him to Lucy's studio. He likes her work, maybe wants to show her.

Get out.

No he really said—

No I mean it, she makes air quotes, "literally." Get the fuck out.

Robin, I'm telling you, nothing happened. We didn't even talk much. I told you I wouldn't. Nothing happened like you think.

So something happened that I didn't think?

Come on, will you give me a break?

You want a break? She holds up the photo, rips it in half, flings it at him, yells, Take your beautiful photo of the beautiful painting of your beautiful body and get the fuck out!

I'm am so tired of this. Of you, your blow-ups. I never know what the hell I'm walking into. What do you want?

I want you to get gone.

Yeah, sure. He shoves the pieces of the photo in his chest pocket, puts his jacket back on. I can do that.

She climbs up on the bed with Benny, pulls him tight to her churning belly as Dan stomps out. She whispers, What do I want? Same thing as always. I want my mother.

Seymour catches Rob coming out of the elevator. Ready? How about I walk over with you.

I'm still on the fence. About going at all.

This one might be worth it. It's only for a couple hours.

She scoffs, does a pretend swoon, But I have nothing to wear.

He crooks his finger, Come inside. I can fix that.

He leads Rob to a black lacquered armoire in one of the bedroom/offices. She had some pretty cool stuff, he murmurs. He turns the key, pulls the door open slowly to reveal a jam-packed row of hanging jackets, coats, kimonos, shawls. You want one?

Rob steps in close, runs her hand over the wool, silk, cotton. Your mother's? You kept all this? All this time?

I don't throw anything out. I just keep it organized so nobody thinks I'm crazy.

She fondles the sleeve of a stark white kimono, whispers, Wow, this is so soft.

Try it on.

You gotta be kidding.

Not as a kimono. Put it on over your stuff, like a jacket.

I can't. I'll rip it. Or spill something. I'll ruin it.

So? It's been sitting here for forever. It's time.

I've never worn anything like it.

That matters?

He takes the garment off the padded hanger, drapes it over her shoulders. She shrinks away from the fabric as if it was made of ice, but it is so smooth, so supple, she gives in and reaches her arms through the wide sleeves. Seymour settles the kimono on top of her turtleneck sweater and jeans. It falls to just below her knees.

Yeah, he says, turning her toward a floor mirror standing in the corner. Look. Beautiful, you look beautiful.

Rob steps toward the glass, shakes her head immediately. Nah, nah, she says, slipping her arms out of the kimono, hands it back. It's too much. I can't.

Seymour rummages in the closet, pulls out a vest, heavily embroidered with metallic threads. Maybe this? See the elephants on it, a symbol of a good memory. And the lining is black, you can reverse it if you change your mind.

Where the hell did that come from?

India, I think. A man's wedding vest.

She puts it on, nods her head. It's heavy. Solid. I don't think I can fuck it up. She spins to look at the back of the vest. "The elephant hath joints, but none for courtesy; his legs are legs for necessity, not for flexure." Strong and clunky. Like me.

I could never figure out *Troilus and Cressida*. I like this one better. "The elephant is never won by anger..." John Wilmot, *Valentinian*. Stole it from Fletcher. So you gonna wear it?

Rob spins around, arms out. Yeah. Why the hell not?

Are you going to the gallery?

That's a different question.

Let's wander by, see.

You'll stay with me?

Dan?

Her eyes tear up, she shakes her head, I don't. He maybe. I wasn't nice again.

He knows you.

I maybe pushed it too far this time.

Always possible.

Rob and Seymour wait across the street, watch for a while. A lone saxophone player is wailing on the sidewalk in front of the gallery. The music complements the city noise—taxis honking, car doors slamming, people mingling, drinking, laughing. The crowd in the gallery forms a blurry vague shadow on the frosted window, like a herd of cattle moving in fog.

How the hell did I ever get here, she whispers.

The hard way. It about killed you to get here.

How do you know?

You're pretty easy to read.

For you maybe. You see things other people don't. Most people just think I'm a bitch. It's gonna be a disaster. Mick can't sell this. Who would want this stuff?

Ay there's the rub. You make it, then you have to find something to do with it. Or else it eats you up.

That's why you sell your boxes for practically nothing in Washington Square?

Nah. I just like watching the chess games. You in?

An art career, she mutters as they walk across the street. All I ever wanted was to play wide receiver for the Giants

A waist-high rectangular perimeter has been created around each room of *Home*, black metal stanchions strung with three rows of barbed wire strands. The furniture is easily visible but unreachable. Seymour heads to get Rob a glass of wine from the bar at the back of the room, Rob hides in a corner watching Stevenson lead a small group from room to room, pointing, pontificating. It's a large crowd, here to see the work as much to scope out the new gallery. Mick is with a red-headed woman near the counter, both looking intently at the brochure of the show. She holds it in the air, compares it to the installation across the room, nods. Melanie comes up with a clipboard, offers the woman a pen. She shakes her head, hands Melanie her wine glass then reaches into her large leather purse and pulls out a fountain pen. She signs the paper clipped to the board with a flourish. Mick smiles, shakes her hand, escorts her to the door. Once she's left, Mick disappears in the crowd and Rob heads into the center of the room. She likes the feel of the wedding vest, the bulk and heaviness reminds her of football shoulder pads. She takes a turn around the installation, listening.

That's her, isn't that her?

Maybe. Yeah. Pretty sure. Got all dolled up again this time.

How the hell did she bend that wire?

It's totally amazing.

It's heavy, the idea that your furniture will hurt you.

Guess there's no place like home.

She's always got some sort of sadness in her work. And some violence.

At least nobody is hitting anything.

Rob laughs to herself, murmurs, Not this time.

Finally! Mick grabs her by the arm. Where the fuck have you been?

I'm here aren't I? What, no Joni?

Did you see me with Cynthia Stanford?

Who?

She works with Alanna Heiss.

The one converting those old buildings?

Yes! This is it. She wants to show *Home* at PS 1.

This is good?

Rob, every artist alive would kill for this! People wait years for a chance like this.

How would I know? So they're gonna buy it?

It's a museum. They exhibit, not purchase. I need to get somebody to buy it. Which will be easy now. Be happy, kiddo. This is truly the big time.

She exhales, relaxes, spins around, showing him the vest. What you think?

Well, well, well, You got dressed up all on your own?

She pushes him away. I just...

No, it's great. I love it. It's you. I'm glad you made the effort.

Over his shoulder, Rob sees Dan having a conversation with a man with his back to her. At least he's not talking to Lucy, she thinks.

Mick goes on, Heiss will be coming tomorrow. You have to meet her. And I want to pitch the piece to Markham.

That moron?

A moron with a ton of cash. Best I do that on my own, yes?

She hears Dan shout, sees him push the man. The man staggers, spins, falls forward into the wire strung between two stanchions. He shrieks as the barbs cut into his hands. The posts fall over, bang against the bed, the bed slides into the chair, sets it rocking. Silence ripples across the room. The man holds up his hands, looks at the tiny punctures, lunges at Dan. Dan wraps his arms around his chest, pulls him in a bear hug, fights to hold him still.

Rob steps to the side, gets a clearer view. Her heart stops. Can't be, can't be, can't be, she whispers, and rushes over and cries out, You told him?

Dan shakes his head. No!

Seymour appears out of nowhere, grabs one of Coach's arms. Coach tries to shrug him off, stumbles. Dan grabs his other arm. They hold him until he is still, then try to walk him out.

Look at her! Coach yells, nodding his head at Rob. My daughter! He sneers, An artist! Who is she kidding.

What the hell is this stuff? ROB? Who the hell do you think you are?

Seymour and Dan usher a resisting Coach through the crowd. As they pass her, she and Coach lock eyes. He yanks them to a halt, sneers at her, says, Artist, my ass. Just like your brother? She gasps, feels it, all of it— the fear, the hate, the need to hurt. She steps toward him, one arm raised high, hand clenched in a fist, brings it down, hard, slaps it into her open palm. Yeah, right, Coach scoffs, That's all you got, isn't it. He charges at her, she stumbles backward. The threads of her vest snag on the wire strung between the stanchions. Mick catches her, pulls her upright before the posts collapse. He helps her take off the vest, untangles it from the wire. Dan and Seymour drag a now quiet Coach out the door.

Mick holds out the vest for Rob. She shakes her head, looks at the frayed threads.

It's not, not so bad, Mick says, Put it back on.

No, no. You keep it. I need to fix—

Go. I can handle this. Go. It will be OK. He smiles, It's gonna be alright, kiddo.

You can't say that.

He hugs her tight, helps her put on the vest. Trust me. I got you, Rob. I got you. The work is fine. Go take care of whatever that is.

As she leaves the building, the crowd re-forms, music resumes. Mick and Melanie adjust the bed, still the rocking chair, right the stanchions.

Always something exciting at a Morgan opening, she hears a woman say as she passes.

Her companion laughs, Doesn't look like that one was planned.

Around the corner, Seymour and Dan have Coach hemmed in near the hood of what Rob recognizes as their old station wagon.

Jesus, Rob says to Dan, Is he drunk?

Yeah, never saw him like this.

Coach yells, Hey ROB, I had to find out where you are from Cassidy's mother?

You didn't looked too hard.

You're the one who took off. No word. After the accident—

I was there for Christ's sake!

He does a double take, Yeah, well. You know. How many years I tried. But never could do anything with him. He was too much like her. He shakes his head, as if to clear it. And what's your problem? We had the plan, the schedule. All you had to do was follow it. It was just like in the army. Simple. Cassidy, what was the problem with them?

Are you serious? The problem is that they weren't soldiers!

Coach turns to Rob, All you had to do was follow the rules. Really. Why was that so hard?

Rob can only stare at him.

Coach turns to Dan, You know me, Danny, you know me. Tell her.

I thought I did, Dan says, I thought I did.

Coach looks from Rob to Dan, his eyes come into focus. You're siding with her? What did she tell you? She'd never—

She did this time, she tells him. How about that. I finally opened my mouth.

Coach steps toward Rob.

Dan pushes him back into the hood of the car, Why were you like that? How could you be such an asshole to them?

Cassidy, what the fuck are you doing here?

I live here, Dan says. With Rob.

Yeah, Rob echoes. We live here. Together.

Come on, Danny. You're smarter than that. Better than that. Didn't I teach you?

Why me? Why not her? Or Jonah?

They never had what you had, your potential—

Fucking football? Dan shakes his head, Really? You cared more about football than your own kids?

They were never really mine.

What the fuck does that mean?

Shit, I may be their father but they were always hers, she made them into what she wanted. I didn't stand a chance. He reaches out, But with you, Danny, you were not like that—

Dan steps back, Don't even try, I got nothing for you. Never will.

Coach's shoulders sag, then he straightens his back, waves his arms as if to make Dan disappear. Well fuck you. Fuck the both of you, he says as he pulls his keys out of his pocket, I don't need either of you.

We can't let him drive, Seymour says, grabbing the keys from Coach's hand.

Let him go, Rob says, let him go. Maybe he'll get hit by a bus too.

Coach springs at her, Danny blocks him with his forearm, he falls back against the car, banging his hip. He sneers at Rob, says, You're still so stupid.

Rob backs up, starts to walk away, has every intention of walking away.

Coach taunts, What a moron. You believed that shit?

She stops, spins, shoves Dan aside, winds up and swings the back of her hand as hard as she can, right across Coach's jaw. His head snaps sideways. As she lifts her arm again, Dan pulls her back.

Coach rights himself, looks her in the eye. So, he whispers, you did learn something. He smiles a smug, satisfied smile. See? See who you are?

Rob clenches her teeth, her hands hang loose at her sides. She starts counting, doesn't realize she is counting out loud. Counts her breaths, then her steps, as she backs away.

Give him the fucking keys, Dan says to Seymour.

I could take him to a hotel, sober him up. I know a place in mid-town.

Just give him the fucking keys. He's not worth it.

Seymour says, I'll drive him.

To New Jersey? Rob says. How will you get back?

On the train. Same way you got here. He opens the back passenger door, waits.

Coach mumbles, spins around. Seymour just stares at him until he climbs into the back seat, grabs the handle and slams the door shut.

Take her home, he says to Dan. I'll see you guys tomorrow.

Jesus, Dan says, I'm gonna kill my mother. What do we do if he comes back?

He won't be back, Rob says quietly.

How do you know?

She sees that smile imprinted on her mind, that satisfied, smug smile. He got what he came for, she says. He'll never be back.

I'm so sorry, Puck, Dan takes her hand as he leads her down the block. I never thought to tell her not to say anything.

So me and Jonah, not his kids. Hers. Jesus. What did he say, in the gallery? Why did you push him?

He kept going on and on, about how me missed me, that he could get me a job as his assistant, that we could be a team again. He wouldn't shut up. I told him I knew, knew about him. Then he did that thing you wrote about, that sneering thing, called me a moron and I couldn't help myself. I wanted to lay him out. I'm sorry I fucked up your show.

Not at all! Good for you. I never had the guts until today. She asks in a small voice, You sure you still want to come with me, live with me?

He stops.

She turns to him, can't look him in the eye. Jesus, Danny. How can you stand me? What I said. About you, Lucy? Before?

Yeah that. That was one of your shittiest ones.

And you put up with that? You shouldn't be so nice. I'm an asshole.

Sometimes. You sure as hell can be. But when you're not—he nods his head in the direction of the street, And I can see how you came by it naturally.

Ain't that the truth. I am. Just like him, aren't I. I try not to be but—

He taps her lightly on the face. And I see it, he says, I see. You try.

I am still gonna be an asshole.

How can you not be, kiddo?

Don't kiddo me. We're not kids any more.

He puts his arm around her shoulders as they resume walking, says quietly, Sometimes it feels like we're both nine hundred years old.

Tell me, Mick says to Dan at breakfast a few weeks later. What's wrong with her? I sold the installation to Markham. She's really rich this time. Getting invited to show at PS 1 is unbelievable. She should be jumping for joy.

Dan laughs, Hard to see Rob jumping for anything.

You know what I mean. Any artist—

Rob comes back to the table. Any artist what?

Mick wants to know why you are not jumping for joy.

She laughs, Me?

That's what I said.

So what is it, kiddo? Why aren't you happy? Your career is taking off gangbusters. Why didn't you show for those interviews Melanie set up?

Jesus, Mick. I'm tired. Maybe just let me alone for a while.

I'm not supposed to let you alone! I'm just trying to do my job—

Yeah, helps you too, she sneers, doesn't it. All the press, all the cash.

Mick tosses his napkin on the table, starts to get up, There she is ladies and gentlemen. Welcome back. There's the old Rob, yes?

She reaches across the table, Wow, Mick, sorry, Mick. Please sit down. It's been—

Was it what happened at the opening, your father showing up like that?

Dan leans in, Maybe you shouldn't—

She lays her hand on his arm, Nah, it's OK. I'm sorry about that. That was, that won't happen again.

It didn't make any difference. To the show. Everything worked out. But what about you? It seemed—

I'm telling you, I'm fine. Just need to be alone. Don't want to talk to anyone, about anything, especially about art.

Dan finishes his coffee, We're thinking about getting out of town for a while.

Yeah, Rob says. A road trip. Just take off, with Benny. For a couple of weeks, maybe longer. I want Dan to meet my friend Jasper first, then we'll leave on Friday.

Mick asks tentatively, But you'll be back for the next show? The next opening?

She punches Dan on the shoulder. Of course! How could I miss the unveiling of naked Dan?

Dan says, We don't have to—

I'm fine, guys, fine with Lucy having a show. It's not my gallery for Christ's sake.

But I—

Nah, really. I'm good with it. She's good. A really good painter. Better than that Thomas guy. And she's got two names like a normal person. I'm over being stupid about it.

Mick nods. Great. Yeah, yeah. Take off for a while. Good idea. I'll be here. When you get back.

Rob smiles, for the first time in two weeks she smiles without seeing Coach's face.

God, Dan says as they enter Jasper's meditation studio, these spaces are fantastic! From the street this building looks like a dump. Is this loft even longer than yours?

Rob nods, Jasper has one of the biggest places I've ever seen. So glad you came, I really want you to meet him. I don't know why I haven't brought you before this. I loved this class, the sun sets during it, the light change is fantastic. Take your shoes off, leave them here.

Come in, come in, Jasper calls from the rear of the loft. He is watering the long row of plants under the windows. It is a grey day, the blue of his pants looks faded in the weak sunlight, his orange shirt dulled. So lovely to see you! Jasper hugs Rob, smiles at Dan. How do you like my buzzer?

Very fancy, Rob says.

Saves me a lot of steps.

If you need it I bet we could fix your elevator.

No need. I'll be moving.

Somewhere uptown?

He shakes his head. Much farther north. I have been invited to teach at an ashram upstate.

You can't!

I can. I am.

What will I do?

Rob, I haven't seen you in ages.

But I need to know you are here, to be here. Always.

Jasper laughs. Did I teach you nothing? Nobody is here always.

Ain't that the truth, Rob mutters, turns to leave. OK, good luck upstate.

Wait, please. Stay. The Wednesday class has been cancelled but I would be happy to have a session with you. And?

Dan, this is my friend Dan.

Jasper bows, Dan smiles.

So you will stay?

Yeah, sure. Why not.

Jasper collects a singing bowl and mallet, sets three cushions in a triangle right in the center of the loft. They each choose a cushion, sit with crossed legs.

Have you ever meditated, Dan?

Yeah, yeah. Some a long time ago and recently with Rob.

Using the bowl?

Rob nods.

Very good. Jasper lays the bowl on his palm, takes up the mallet.

What should we focus on? Rob asks.

How about you choose for yourself this time, Jasper says. Perhaps think about what is uppermost in your mind, in your heart.

He taps the bowl three times. As the tones begin to fade, he sends the mallet around the rim in a slow, even rhythm. Dan gives a small grunt, rounds his shoulders, breathes deeply. Rob has trouble falling into the sounds, her mind is all over her place, full of sadness that Jasper is leaving, angry at herself for trusting he would be there, angry at herself for being angry about that. The encounter with Coach left her on a sharp edge, constantly watching herself, monitoring her behavior. She can't shake that sneering smile, the knowledge that she is, despite all her effort, just like him. She struggles to clear her head, to keep from falling into counting, and finally just gives in, allows the tones take her. She follows the sounds, rising, floating. Then, with no warning, she is in free-fall.

the man pounds on the bathroom door, the jamb splinters as the lock gives way. a woman is lying in the overflowing tub. she holds a small boy in her bleeding arms. the man snatches the boy from her. take him! he shouts to the girl beside him. take him and get out! she hears the woman's voice. remember, Puck. for I love you so, that I in your sweet thoughts would be forgot, if thinking on me then should make you woe. fucking Shakespeare? the man shouts. he clamps his hands on the woman's bloody arms, snarls at the girl. I said get out!

Rob gasps, opens her eyes, whispers, No, no, no, no no, then jumps to her feet, runs to the door, stuffs her feet into her boots. The door slams as she tears down the stairs.

Jasper sets the bowl and mallet into his lap. Rob?

Dan opens his eyes. Puck, where the hell are you going?

It's nearly midnight. Dan and Seymour stand on the corner of Greene and Prince. Benny paces nervously in front of them.

Now where? Seymour asks. Not at the park, or the courts.

I was sure she'd be on Tenth Street, Dan says, at her old house. Is it time to call the cops?

Benny barks, strains on the leash, lunges toward the street.

Of course, Seymour says and lets go of the lead. Why didn't we just send you to find her.

Benny jumps, his paws land on Rob's shoulders. She wraps her arms around his neck. Dan starts towards her. Seymour shakes his head, holds him back. Rob is soaked. And filthy. Her hair is plastered to her head—her face, hands, jeans, sweater, boots—everything covered with wet, sooty dirt.

It's not bad, really. Not as bad as it looks, she says, handing Benny's leash to Dan.

He takes it, settles the dog next to him, says, So you ran away to become a chimney sweep?

Rob looks up, tries to smile, starts to cry.

Too soon, Seymour says, too soon. He takes her hand, leads her to the elevator. Come on, you might need a bath.

She sits silently at the kitchen table, absently petting Benny.

Seymour throws wood into the stove, stokes the fire. Dan runs water into the tub, says to Seymour, I got this, man. Thanks.

Seymour takes Rob's hand, squeezes it, releases it, You know where I am.

Rob is still, compliant like a sleepy child. Dan removes her boots, unbuttons her pants, slides them off. When he pulls her sweater over her head he sees a jagged cut on her forearm. She barely notices as he wipes off the dried blood, the mud. He walks her across the room, next to the tub.

I have to?

It's OK, It's OK, I am here.

She closes her eyes, lets him help her step into the tub. She crouches, will not lay down. He soaps up a cloth, washes her face and neck, her arms and hands. Takes great care with the wound. The tub fills with oily, dirty water.

Come with me, he says softly as he reaches under her arms, lifts her from the tub, wraps her in a towel. We can wash your hair in the sink.

Why didn't you wake me? How long have I been asleep?

Dan throws a couple of scraps into the stove, Almost a day. You hungry?

We got any more of that good wine?

He pours a cupful, says, You conked out, after the bath. Seymour was here, checked on your arm. He said you've had a tetanus shot not long ago? Mick came over this morning and Jasper came by a while ago to see how you were. I couldn't wake you. It was like you were drugged. He holds up a faded, frayed shirt, Jasper left this for you, something about orange being healing. And your sketchbook, you ran out without it.

She takes the shirt, holds it up to the light, sets it in her lap. Runs her hand over the top of the book says quietly, It's so stupid, so embarrassing. I am such an idiot. I talked myself into believing I was seeing things I had never seen, hearing her say stuff I had never heard. Jasper told me, but I wouldn't believe him. And like an even bigger idiot I wanted more, tried to hear more, see more. And then, there it was. There it was. I couldn't pretend I never heard it, never saw it. I was there.

She winds Jasper's shirt around her hands, notices the bandage on her arm.

Dan sits, reaches his arms across the table. She retreats. He points to the bandage.

Did you?

He lied. Lied through his stinking teeth. Every day.

There was no fucking bus accident. That's what he was talking about, when he showed up. Who gets hit by a bus except in a joke! She did it to herself. My mother killed herself. I think she was trying to kill Jonah. I had to have known. But didn't want to know that I knew. Everything I told myself my whole fucking life has been a big fat lie.

He repeats. Did you?

She looks at the bandage, holds her arm up, away from her body. No, no, she says quickly. No it's not that. It's no big deal. It's almost, no it's actually funny, you will think it's funny.

He gives her the side eye, pours himself more wine. We went looking for you, me and Seymour. Where were you?

She picks up Jasper's shirt, rubs it against her cheek. Everybody leaves, she murmurs. Benny brushes against her legs, sits under her chair. Except you.

And me, Dan says quietly.

You don't know that.

Actually I do. He holds up a copy of the NY Times, reads the headline, "Last Draft Call December 7th."

What's today?

November 18th. Highest number so far was 215. No way they are getting to me in a couple of weeks.

Jesus! I feel like Rip Van Winkle. Is that true? You aren't gonna leave?

So you OK? He points to the cut on her arm again. Tell me. Where were you?

Long story, but I ended up at the piers, where I found the wood I've been using.

Yeah, but how did you get that on your arm?

OK OK. After I left Jasper's, I started running, planned to run all the way to Penn Station. Hop a train, confront the bastard. After about ten blocks I could barely breathe. I should maybe quit smoking. I started walking. Thinking. What did I need to talk to him for? All he'd do is call me a moron again. I already knew I was a moron. What would I get from him but more grief. So it's getting dark, I'm walking and walking and I realize that I'm counting. But I don't want to count, this time I want to remember. I head over to the west side, to the place I know really well, and go over it in my head, again and again. What I saw at the session with Jasper. She killed herself, Danny. My mother slit her wrists in the bathtub in our house on Tenth Street. She locked the door. She had Jonah, in the tub with her. You know what that means?

Jesus. Yes. What happened?

He was there. Coach. He broke the door down. Grabbed Jonah, shoved him at me. I guess he called the cops or an ambulance. That's all I remember. No not all. She said something to me. Told me to remember it. Fucking Shakespeare.

Do you? Remember?

Yeah, I remember. But it was bullshit.

How so?

Rob sits up tall, tries to recite, but her voice cracks. For I love you so, that I in your sweet thoughts would be forgot, if thinking on me then should make you woe. The end of sonnet seventy-one.

So she was saying—

She was fucking saying that I should remember to forget her!

Dan says drily, I can see how that would be confusing.

Rob scoffs, Right? I knew you'd get it. So I'm sitting on this busted pier, the river washing back and forth under my feet. And I am getting madder and madder. I start howling. Actually howling! Screaming loud enough to scare off the goddamned rats. And I don't know who I hate more. Her or Coach. Who I want to kill more. Or first. But she's already dead, right? And what good would it do to kill him? She takes a big swig of wine. Did you ever see Titus Andronicus?

You giving me more Shakespeare?

Yeah, yeah, but. Something Grace said. About emulation—how the cycle of revenge is beyond stupid, gets you nowhere but eaten by a lion.

I might have to read that play.

She laughs, Only you.

Your arm?

Jesus, OK. I'm getting to it. So now it's really dark. No streetlights, but the moon is full enough so I can see a little. I don't know why I didn't just come home, but I couldn't move. It's getting really cold. I stick my hand in my pants pocket, and there it is. The knife she gave me. Her father's knife. The knife I used to cut a guy who tried to rape me. The knife I made my first real sculpture with. I hold it in my hand, my open hand, stare at it. I hate this knife. I love this knife. And now I start remembering for real. All the times it was good with her, but also all the times it wasn't. She really was kind of crazy, way more Ophelia than Ariel. And I don't think she liked me. Loved me, probably, but not sure about like. Always wanting to change me, dress me, telling me how I could be prettier. She made me wear a dress to see a play. I hated dresses! But she wouldn't let me go unless I put on some stupid dress. And now I hate Shakespeare! I don't want to hate Shakespeare!

Rob is laugh/crying. Dan tosses her a dish towel.

And then the kicker, she goes on. I heard. Remembered. How she was always saying I was too much like him. That I had to be different, more like Jonah. So now all I want to do is get rid of the goddamned knife. Her gift. Get her out of my mind. I stand up to make this grand gesture, pull my arm back to fling it into the middle of the river and the fucking thing slips off my palm, right below my feet. It's in the water, just sitting there. I can just about see it, it's not that deep. And I change my mind, realize that I want to keep it. Why should I just throw it away? So I roll up my sleeve, reach in to grab it and there's this sharp pain. I get cut on a nail sticking out of the piling. Not a big cut, but it starts bleeding, the stinking river water getting in it, so I yank my arm out as hard and fast as I can and I fell. Backwards. Off the pier into the water, a backwards belly flop. Not too deep but deep enough to get all of me wet, get the creosote crusty sooty wet crap all over me.

Fucking Shakespearean.

She starts to laugh again. Starts to cry.

So did you get it? The knife?

No, she says, wiping her nose. I gave up on it.

He nods, refills her wine cup. I'll get you one. I'll get you a new knife.

It's weird. I get it now, about why Coach was so hard on Jonah. He looked like her, acted like her—

That's not even close to being an excuse—

Nah, nah. For sure no excuse. I still hate the bastard. But it helps somehow, helps me, that it makes sense. And Danny, Dan. No more Puck. I'm done being Puck.

We're running out of names here. What do I call you, when I want to be sweet? Who do you want to be?

No idea. Yet.

Jasper comes in to the loft. Rob? You in here? Dan let me up.

Yeah, she yells, come in. In the back. Rob is sitting on the kitchen floor, brushing Benny. Take a seat, I'll be done in a sec and make some tea. You like Lapsang Souchong?

I do. Very much. And I love your place, the studio, and back here, cozy, like a mountain cabin.

I'll be sorry to give it up. Just a sublet. The owners are supposed to be back at the beginning of next year.

And then?

She shrugs, fills a teapot with hot water from the kettle on the wood stove, sets an empty mug on the table in front of him.

He cups his hands around the warming teapot, looks down, says, I'll be moving north tomorrow, Rob. I've come to say goodbye.

Yeah, I know. I'm trying not to feel ditched, but I'm happy—

And I have a confession. He pours tea into their cups. Rob, I breached your trust.

What does that even mean?

He raises his head, looks her in the eye. I read your notebook without asking. You left it when you took off. I feel terrible.

She gets up, breaks up some kindling for the stove. If you think that's terrible—you did read what I wrote, didn't you?

I never meant to. Wow, that's lame. I just opened it, read a few sentences. I was really intrigued. Just kept going.

So you read the whole thing?

He nods.

Jesus Christ!

You have every right to be mad.

I'm not mad. Not very. I'm embarrassed!

What for?

Now you know! Me. What I was. What I did. What I am.

He nods, And I also know why.

Big fucking deal! I know why now too. So I should be able to stop. Right? But I'm still doing it! Like right now! It's what I am. I'll never be different.

What happened to you, Rob, how you got like this, took years. Building up day after day. Hating. Being afraid. Stuffing it, deeper and deeper into your body. It's in your bones, but it got put there. It's not who you are, it has just been shoved so deep down. It's not simply going away because you can name it, talk about it.

How the fuck do you know so much about it?

He stands up, puts his hand on his heart, says in a mock friendly voice, Hi! My name is Jasper and I'm an Anger-a-holic.

Cool, calm, collected Jasper?

Oh yeah. For me it was my mother. She was a drunk, a vile, mean drunk. When she wasn't totally out of it she yelled, screamed, undercut, belittled me. All day, every day. Me and my older brother.

You have a brother?

Had. He got out by joining the army. Died in Korea.

Oh man.

I'm really sorry about your brother, Rob. It sounds like he was a great kid.

She takes a deep breath, shakes her head. Not now, she whispers, not yet. What about your father?

No idea. Never knew him. I always had this fantasy, that she was such a bitch she drove him away. That if she had been different I would have had one big happy family. Took years of meditating to get rid of that one.

My mother killed herself. Left us alone with him.

He nods, Dan told me.

He did?

He was worried. I was worried. We were both so worried.

She laughs, My boys. Thanks, yeah, thanks, really thank you. She takes a small sip of tea. So, my diary, will I win the Pulitzer?

If they gave one for bravery maybe.

Brave. That's what Danny said. That I was brave to make the barbed wire stuff. To show it. What's so brave about it?

You're not hiding anymore.

But it's not working, I'm still—

You're aware of it, you care about fixing it. You're miles ahead of where I was at your age. Took me close to twenty years to get there.

How?

Meditation.

I hate sitting still. I only did it because I was stupid. Thought I heard my mother.

You're mad at her now too?

Yeah! No. I don't know. What's the point? She looks up, eyes tearing. Benny jumps off the bed, lays his head on her lap. What the hell am I supposed to do?

You are so good with the bowl.

Got the magic touch, she scoffs.

He nods, Sort of. You do have empathy, a ton of empathy. Dan said you helped him find some clarity with something? Why don't you come with me to the ashram?

I'm a city girl, Jasper, don't do bugs, wild animals.

Then find another group here in town.

Nah. You know me, not so great with people.

True. So just keep going. On your own.

And it will help how?

He laughs, The fuck if I know. I just know it does.

When Donald and Maria return in February, Dan and Rob move down to the second floor. They set up a kitchen in the back, live on Seymour's *Road to Rio* furniture in the front of the loft. Seymour evicts the textile company tenants, helps Dan set up a studio on the third floor. After two weeks of vacuuming up thousands of tiny pieces of fabric, millions of threads, the space is clean, streamlined. Dan builds simple wooden benches that are now full of electrical wires, plugs, batteries, microphones, earphones, cigar boxes labeled in black marker, and piles of cassette tapes and recorders. Rob has done nothing since the work for *Home*, hasn't even looked for new studio space. Uncharacteristically, Mick waits. Doesn't badger her.

Hey what's that sound? Rob asks. You using my bowl?

Dan pops a microcassette out of the recorder. I taped it, last time you were using it.

Sounds pretty good, she says. Not the same, but pretty good.

So you ready?

We're really gonna do this.

Yep. Dinner and a movie, like normal people.

It's such a cliché. Remind me why.

Because we never did.

I feel like a teen-ager.

Exactly! You never got to be a teen-ager.

We can't go back—

I know that. But Seymour says we can go forward.

Seymour says. A whole lot of Seymour says. He like your new coach or something?

Jeez Rob, it's not a bad thing. To have someone like that in your life.

I get it. I'm just not used to it. You're right. Seymour's the man. For me too. So Danny, we going on a date? Dan?

I can see you're still having trouble. How about I just be Danny again.

She hands Benny a treat, settles him onto the bed, Would I have to be Puck?

Only if you want. He helps her on with her jacket, I get points for this, you know.

I'm not taking any Cosmo Quiz.

I would pay big money to read your answers.

Rob toys with the pile of wires while Dan cleans the heads of one of the tape recorders lined up on his bench.

Where do you get them all?

Mostly from this guy on Canal Street. He taught me how to fix them.

You taping stuff, like all the time?

He nods, I love it. You'd be amazed at what I hear, what's out there, the sounds changing, blending. Just standing in the same place. All I have to do is stop, listen. I must have a couple hundred tapes so far. I just started figuring out how to splice them. And make loops.

Jonah made tape loops. He was really good.

Dan nods, I miss him too.

She winces, feels the pain without needing to escape it. So what are you gonna do with them all?

He shakes his head. No idea.

You still have that one? The one of the singing bowl?

He pulls out the cigar box marked, Bowl Tapes. Sure, right here.

Can I listen again?

Yeah, yeah. He pops the cassette into a micro recorder, pushes play, hands it to her.

Wait wait. Turn it off a second. You got anything metal around here?

Empty tool chest?

Yeah, yeah, good. Is this the loudest? As high as it goes?

Yeah, max volume.

She sets the recorder on the bench, pushes play, then places lid of the chest over the recorder, props up the edge with a D battery. They listen, until the tape stops. The metal somehow deepens the tones, it nearly sounds like an actual bowl session. Dan upends the tool chest, pulls out the tape, starts to put it back in the box.

Rob jumps up, Wait! Lemme see that? She tosses the cassette back and forth as she paces in front of the bench. Hey! Wow. That sound. Is that the smallest recorder? Can you use batteries? Or do you have to plug it in?

There's lots of recorders, different sizes, different kinds.

Did you like that? Did it sound good to you? Like it really sounds?

Almost, almost. Yeah. It sounded good.

We'd have to play with different ideas for it. Find out what works best, come up with something to house the recorder.

We?

Yeah! We could do something. Do something together.

Where?

She looks around his space. Yeah, I'd need to get a studio. Maria wants me to move all my crap out soon anyway.

You could probably rent upstairs, the 4th floor?

Maybe. But I really miss being able to get on the roof. Remember Jasper's place?

How could I forget that.

It's for sale.

The loft?

The whole building.

Whoa.

It's only a three story. I could rent out the bottom floors. Split the top floor in two, like we had upstairs here.

You got that kind of money?

I do have that kind of money. Thanks to all those heads and my favorite moron Markham. But nobody will give me a mortgage. Seymour said he'd help figure it out. Everything around here is still pretty cheap. But Mick thinks not for long. He's looking to buy the building the gallery is in.

It seems like such a grown-up thing. Buying a building.

She laughs. I'm feeling it, feeling grown up. So, do you wanna? Work with me?

He shrugs, wipes oil from his hands. Maybe. I don't know. Maybe.

Only maybe? Maybe?

Is it gonna be like when you made the furniture for *Home*?

Like?

I don't think I want to be around that. If you get like you did. For us to get like we did. Isolated, distant. You yelling all the time. Us having mediocre sex.

She feels a flash of anger, breathes till it passes then sits on a stool, shrugs, says quietly, Yeah. I get it. Get why you wouldn't want a re-do of that. I can't promise. It could. I could, get like that. I don't know. But maybe this is different. This feels different. Maybe I'm different. At least a little. I think this is going to be, God help me Danny, this could actually be sort of happy somehow. Maybe even peaceful.

He laughs, sits next to her. Happy? You?

It could. Maybe it's time.

So we would be that kind of a we? An artist we?

I can see it. Can't you?

What the hell, Puck. It's worth a shot.

She whispers, Puck, huh. Yeah, alright. It's time. I'm good. I can be Puck again.

Then yeah, for sure let's give it a shot, he says again as he lays out five different recorders. So what are you thinking?

No idea. Some kind of container for the recorder, so you don't see the machine but you can make it play. Hear it. Definitely some kind of metal.

Like a bowl?

Nah, not a bowl. Something closed in. A globe. Or a box. Yeah, probably a box, you know, like a music box.

Big? Like an installation?

No. I want to make them so people can have one. At home. Hear it when they want to. Need to. Each one will be a tape of a different bowl session. We can set up booth-like spaces in the gallery, like sound booths, so people can listen to them, choose one.

We could do that with ear phones. Make it a lot cleaner, simpler.

Yes! I'll have to learn a lot about metal. We'll have to try a bunch of metals. The sounds have to ring, really resonate.

And fade, he says. The ending is key, where it fades out. It has to go to that place where it's still. We have to take it to silence.

She nods, Yeah. To that place where you can actually hear yourself.

ACKNOWLEDGEMENTS

Thanks to Ellis Amdur, Martha Glenn, Tad Glenn, Dana Harris-Trovato, Riki Moss and Pat Phoebus for comments and encouragement. For everything else, thanks to Madison Smartt Bell.

Kini Collins has spent her life as an artist—
martial, visual, literary. Day jobs to support
those habits include event producer, book store
manager, gallery assistant, community organizer,
dog walker, nanny, teacher and office temp. Raised
in central New Jersey in the 1960s she finally
settled in Baltimore in 1998 after a whole lot of
stops along the way. She lives with an astonishingly
supportive, caring wife and a small dog.